"Miss Archibald, I will say it again. This is no place for a woman."

Before he could escape, Jenny spoke. "I'll leave when I deem it's appropriate, but I won't be run off. I won't be scared off. So don't even try."

He turned slowly. "Don't flatter yourself that I'd bother. You'll find plenty of challenges without my interference."

What on earth did he mean? Was there some sort of danger she should be aware of?

But he was gone before she could ask.

She heard the sound of horse hooves and looked out the window in time to see Burke riding away, leaning forward as if anxious to be away from this place. She shivered. Should she be afraid of him?

He turned, saw her at the window. His gaze drilled into her, dark, powerful, full of—

She jerked back and pressed her palm to her throat.

Promise? Hope? Or was it a warning?

Books by Linda Ford

Love Inspired Historical

The Road to Love
The Journey Home
The Path to Her Heart
Dakota Child
The Cowboy's Baby
Dakota Cowboy
Dakota Father

LINDA FORD

shares her life with her rancher husband, a grown son, a live-in client she provides care for and a yappy parrot. She and her husband raised a family of fourteen children, ten adopted, providing her with plenty of opportunity to experience God's love and faithfulness. They had their share of adventures, as well. Taking twelve kids in a motor home on a three-thousand-mile road trip would be high on the list. They live in Alberta, Canada, close enough to the Rockies to admire them every day. She enjoys writing stories that reveal God's wondrous love through the lives of her characters.

Linda enjoys hearing from readers. Contact her at linda@lindaford.org or check out her website at www.lindaford.org, where you can also catch her blog, which often carries glimpses of both her writing activities and family life.

LINDA FORD
Dakota Father

Steeple
Hill®

Published by Steeple Hill Books™

STEEPLE HILL BOOKS

Steeple
Hill®

Recycling programs
for this product may
not exist in your area.

ISBN-13: 978-0-373-82852-4

DAKOTA FATHER

www.SteepleHill.com

Printed in U.S.A.

I will praise thee; for I am fearfully and wonderfully made.

—*Psalm* 139:14

To my grandparents and great-grandparents,
who faced challenges in moving to a new land.
I am in awe of the hardships they endured and
conquered. We owe them, and the pioneers like them,
a debt of gratitude.

Chapter One

Buffalo Hollow, Dakota Territory, 1884

Nineteen-year-old Jenny Archibald spared a moment to dab at her forehead. If only she could escape the heat sucking at her pores and driving two-year-old Meggie to fretfulness. Jenny sensed the annoyance of those who shared the passenger rail car, cooped up in the same hot box as she and Meggie and having to endure the fitful cries of a child.

She pulled a clean cloth from the valise at her feet and spread it over the leather seat across from her. "Meggie, lie down and I'll fan you." They'd both be considerably cooler if Meggie didn't clutch at her neck and struggle in her arms.

Meggie whined a protest but allowed Jenny to put her down and, as she promised, Jenny waved over the child the book she had hoped to read on the trip.

She'd naively thought Meggie would sleep the entire way from Center City, Ohio, or be happy to stare out the window at the passing scenery.

After a few minutes of fussing, Meg stuck two fingers in her mouth and her eyelids lowered. Jenny let out a sigh of relief. And hid a smile as the other occupants let out echoing sighs.

She glanced about the car. Apart from a withered old lady mumbling in the far seat, Jenny was the only woman aboard. Across the aisle sat two men who seemed to be business associates. They had persevered in wearing their suit coats for the first hour of the trip but now had shed them and waved paper before their faces trying to cool themselves.

Further along, a cowboy hunched over, his legs stretched out beside the seat in front of him. He spared her a sharp look then pulled his hat low and let his chin fall to his chest.

Jenny told herself she would not look at the man who sat across from the old lady. She'd been aware of him since he joined them several stops back—dressed in black, with black hair, and black eyes that seemed to see everything.

Pa was right when he said to her, "Pepper, you must learn to restrain your impulses. Think before you leap."

Only it wasn't that she exactly jumped at the sight of the man. Or the thought of him sitting there so calm and self-contained. More like her heart did a funny little jerk and her eyes jolted to him and away as if controlled by a power beyond her mind.

Like now. Despite her best intentions, she glanced at him. He watched her, his eyes bottomless. Her breath caught in a pool of heat somewhere behind her heart and she couldn't look away.

It took Meggie's wail to free her from his intense stare.

"Mama. I want Mama."

Jenny's heart ached for this child. How could she begin to comprehend the loss of both parents? As Lena and Mark lay dying of the raging fever that had taken so many lives Jenny promised them she would see their child delivered to Lena's brother and his wife and stay long enough to see her settled.

She did her best to soothe Meggie and fan her without resorting to picking her up.

The men across the aisle sighed. One muttered loudly enough for the whole car to hear. "You'd think people would know enough to teach their children how to behave in public."

Jenny stung under the unfair criticism. Meggie wasn't her child but even if she had been, the child could be excused her crankiness. No doubt she felt the heat even more than the rest of them.

If only she could find some cool refreshing water for her. She'd tasted the water from the jug at the back. It was hot and smelled funny. All she needed was for Meg to take sick. But even that inadequate supply had disappeared a short time ago.

The conductor assured her they would soon reach Buffalo Hollow where she could find fresh water before the next stage of her journey.

The muttering of the old woman increased in volume. She was clearly annoyed with Meggie's fussing. The slouching cowboy sat up straight, pushed his hat back and fixed Jenny with a belligerent look.

"Needs a good whupping."

Tears stung the back of Jenny's eyes. She blinked them back, tossed her head and pursed her lips. She would not let their comments affect her.

"Leave her be. The kid's as hot and cranky as the rest of us." The low words from the black-clad man made Jenny's tongue stick to the roof of her mouth. If only she could find a drink.

She glanced at the speaker, again felt that funny sensation deep in her heart. Knowing her feelings were spilling from her eyes, she ducked her head.

Guilt stung her ears. She'd promised Pa to return as quickly as she could, promised she would then hear Ted's offer of marriage. It was only a formality. Ma and Pa both highly approved of Ted Rusk who worked with Pa in the store. When Jenny protested she didn't feel like settling down despite her age, Ma cautioned, "Jenny, you must learn to think with your head not your heart."

"Ted is steady," Pa said. "He'll settle you down."

They knew what was best for her. And didn't the scripture instruct her to honor her father and mother? She intended to obey God's word. Didn't intend to follow her foolish heart into any more disasters.

Both parents had given cautious consent to her plan to take Meggie to Lena's family. No doubt they figured this adventure would get her restlessness out of her system.

She hoped it would, that she'd be ready to take her role as Ted's wife and partner as she intended to. Having given her word, she would fulfill it. Her word was her bond. She would learn to still the restless voice whispering from the dark corners of her imagination. She knew too well the risks of listening to that voice and would never again do so.

Meggie wouldn't settle and begged to be held. They were both sticky with heat but Jenny gathered the baby in her arms and rocked her, crooning soothing sounds which did little to ease Meggie's fussing and nothing to ease Jenny's feeling of being watched.

Stealing a glance from under her eyelashes, she saw the dark-eyed man studying her, a tightness about his mouth. He realized she looked at him and nodded, giving a smile that barely widened his mouth and pushed the tightness upward to his eyes. Yet he didn't look so much disapproving as simply hot and tired like the rest of them.

She nodded, her own smile small and polite even though inside she felt such an unusual touch of excitement. Again she ducked her head and studied the back of the bench before her.

Lord, I have promises to keep. I have tasks to do. And You know me. I have a side of me that rebels, overreacts, enjoys a breathless gallop. She thought of the verse Ma had drilled into her head and heart, 'Godliness with contentment is great gain.' There was no point in longing for things she couldn't have. She tried to find contentment even as she wondered that God had made her a woman—one who must abide by the tight restraints of society when she longed to be free to explore and adventure. She smiled as she thought of how she had—in the not so distant past— tried to talk Pa into heading for the Black Hills to look for gold.

Pa laughed. "Pepper, don't let the glitter of gold make you blind to the beauty of stability."

She loved Pa. He understood her better than anyone, perhaps even better than she understood herself. That's why she'd promised she and Ted would be engaged as soon as she returned. Pa approved of Ted and thought he would be the perfect mate for her. She trusted Pa's love and wisdom.

The conductor came through the car calling, "Buffalo Hollow next stop." He paused at Jenny's side. "I'll help you with the little one when we get there."

Her insides did a tumble as she thought of what faced her. She must find transportation to Lena's brother's ranch and turn Meggie over to the man and his wife. She would see Meggie settled as she promised then return home. But—she allowed a trickle of excitement—the settling-in period would surely give her a chance to explore the countryside. Just the thought made her shift so she could watch out the window. The golden prairie drifted past. The sky seemed endless, making her feel small yet light, as if she could float forever under the blue canopy.

The train jerked to a halt, puffing and groaning. The old woman muttered about having to endure the ride longer. All the men rose and headed for the door. Only the black-haired man paused to indicate she should precede him.

Flustered at his kindness, she fumbled to pull the two traveling bags from the overhead rack—an impossible task with Meggie clutched in her arms. She tried to put Meggie on her feet so she could manage but Meggie clung to her and refused to stand.

Jenny grew even warmer as the man patiently waited.

"I'll take your bags. You carry the child."

She managed to untangle her thoughts enough to

murmur "thank you," then hurried down the aisle and let the conductor assist her to the platform.

The stranger set her bags on the wooden platform. He considered her with a dark intense look. "Ma'am, if I might give you some advice?"

She nodded.

"Go home. This is no place for a woman and child." He tipped his head in good-bye and strode away.

"Go home?" she sputtered, but he continued on without a backward glance. No place for a woman and child? Who was he to make such a statement? Lena said her brother had sent for his intended six months ago. That woman had come out—no doubt happily married by now. Besides—she sniffed—did he think women were too fragile for frontier life? Too fussy? Too soft? She sniffed again. She could prove him wrong if he cared to hang about and see.

But of course he didn't and would never know how she would welcome the challenge of this life if it were offered to her. However, that wasn't going to happen. She would deliver Meggie and return home to her stable life. But not—she glared at the place where the man had disappeared from sight—because she couldn't stand the challenge of living out West.

As Burke Edwards rode from town he restrained the urge to lean forward and gallop all the way home.

He wouldn't find any sense of peace and release until he could shed his Sunday-go-to-town clothes for jeans and chaps, and ride out on the prairie. He'd wished for a different outcome to his trip though in the back of his mind he knew the futility of hope. Had known, he supposed, from the first, but he had fought it. Perhaps if he'd accepted it from the beginning, made the necessary changes, all this would have turned out differently.

He sighed and settled back into the saddle, letting the rhythm of riding and the familiar scents and sights of the open prairie soothe his troubled mind.

Unbidden, unwelcome, his thoughts turned back to his recent train ride.

He'd noticed the girl the minute he got on the train—her hair trailing in damp disarray from the roll coiled about her head, her bonnet askew as the baby batted at it, her brown eyes both weary and patient. When he sat facing her he saw how her smiling brown eyes darted about, taking in everything. He admired her for coping with the fussy little girl, for smiling and nodding politely when the other passengers complained of the noise.

But the way she peered out the window in awe brought such a surge of heat to his brain, he'd seen stars. He wanted to tell her, yup, that's what most of Dakota Territory was like—flat, endless prairie. Great for cows and horses. Deadly for women.

He'd studied her. Held her gaze steadily when she glanced his way. In that moment he'd felt something promising, even hopeful as if she dared him to venture into the unknown with him.

Just remembering that fleeting sensation made him snort. "I guess I've learned my lesson," he muttered to the silent prairie and uninterested horse. This was no place for a woman. He'd told her so then marched away without giving her a chance to reply.

A smile lifted the corners of his mouth. Her eyes had fired up a protest. She'd sputtered. Would have argued if he'd given her opportunity. If he hadn't learned his lesson a little too well he might have paused long enough to see her let off steam. Instead he marched away. Heard her words of protest follow. Had to steel himself not to turn and satisfy his desire to see how she looked all het up.

For a moment he wondered at her destination. He knew most people from the area who did business at Buffalo Hollow. Hadn't heard of anyone expecting a visitor. From what he'd overheard the woman explain to the conductor, this was more than a visit. She'd said something about joining an uncle. He'd heard her mention the child's father dying from a fever and guessed she was a widow.

He shrugged. He'd not see her again, of that he was certain. He only hoped she'd heed his words of warning and leave this country before it destroyed her.

The thoughts he'd been trying to avoid all afternoon flooded his mind, tearing up his plans, his dreams, his future. He'd known it was coming but had refused to accept it. But today had been final. The words left no room for doubt or hope. At twenty-five years of age, he, Burke Edwards, knew his future would take a different shape than the one he'd had in mind when he headed West three years ago with big ideas and bigger dreams.

The ranch came in sight. The house was intended to provide a home for a growing family. It would not happen now. Or ever. The house was only partially finished. He'd intended to extend it further to create a large front room where he and his growing family would gather in the dusk of the evening and enjoy each other's company. He figured there would be a woman in a rocking chair knitting or mending, he in another chair reading the paper or making plans for the future and someday, children at his feet or on his lap. Knowing it would never happen didn't make it easy to push those imaginations into the distance, never to be revisited.

Guess he'd known what the final outcome would be because he had abandoned all pretense of work on the house several months ago. It no longer bothered him that it looked forlorn and neglected. He would probably never complete it. No need to. It was adequate for his purposes.

He reined back to study the place and analyze his feelings. Shouldn't he feel something besides disappointment that there was no reason to finish the house? Shouldn't he be mourning the fact he and Flora would never marry?

"Guess I've known it for a long time. I've just been going through the motions of asking, waiting, hoping because I knew that's what I should do. But you know what, horse? I expect I'm happy enough to let it go. In some ways it's better that it is over and final." Still he couldn't quite shake a sense of failure. He should have walked away from the ranch when he'd seen how Flora felt about it. He didn't need her parents pointing out that her present condition and her current incarceration in the insane asylum was due, in no small part, to his failure to do so.

He flicked the reins and rode into the yard, turning toward the barn. He dropped to the ground. "Lucky," he called to the squat little man hanging around the corrals, wielding a pitchfork. The man was past his prime, one leg all gimped up from an accident. But he was handy around the place and had proven to be a loyal friend. "Look after my horse."

"Okay, Boss." He dropped the fork and sprinted over to take the reins. "Good trip, Boss?"

"Glad to be home."

Lucky chuckled. "Absence makes the heart grow fonder, they say."

"What's new around here?" He'd only been away two days but it felt like a month.

"Nothing, Boss. Though Mac said he thought the spring over to the west was drying out."

"I'll ride over tomorrow and check."

"And the mosquitoes been awful bad. I'm about to start a smudge over past the barn for the horses."

"I'll do it." Burke welcomed the chance to be out in the open doing something mindless and undemanding. He didn't want to think of Flora or his failures. He smiled as he recalled the look on the young woman's face as he warned her this territory was too tough for a woman, then he shook his head.

He didn't want to think about her, either.

His restlessness returned with a vengeance matching the vicious prairie winds. "Lucky, throw my saddle on another mount. I'll ride out and have a look at things." He strode to the house with an urgency that had no cause and quickly changed into his comfortable work clothes. He paused long enough to build the smudge, smeared some lard on the back of his neck to protect himself and rode into the wide open spaces where a man could enjoy forgetfulness.

Forgetfulness was all he sought—all he needed.

* * *

Jenny jolted to one side as the buggy bounced along the trail. She feared little, hadn't blinked when caring for Meggie's parents in their final days. Nor had she felt anything but a trickle of excitement at the task they had given her before their death—deliver their child to her new guardian. But trepidation gnawed into her bones as the miles passed. She'd soon have to meet Lena's brother and his wife and inform them of Lena and Mark's deaths, then turn Meggie over to their care.

Jenny smiled at the child in her arms. It was appreciably cooler riding in the open buggy and Meggie had fallen asleep. She loved this little girl. It would be a wrench to leave her.

"How much farther?" she asked the man she'd hired to take her to the ranch in the far corner of the Dakotas.

"Lookee there and you can see the buildings in the distance."

She followed the direction he indicated and indeed, saw a cluster of buildings. "Looks almost as big as Buffalo Hollow." The little prairie town had proved dusty and squat but friendly. The store owner had allowed her to wash Meggie and tidy them both up as best she could. Customers had offered greetings and given her details about the ranch she was about to reach.

"Big place."

"Boss works his men hard and himself harder."

"Too bad about what happened."

When she pressed for details on that latter bit of information she found the people of Buffalo Hollow suddenly reticent.

Too bad? A fire perhaps or a broken bone.

Now, as she studied the far-off buildings, she wished she'd insisted someone tell her what they meant. She could almost hear Pa's voice and she smiled up into the sky. 'Pepper, you must learn to guard your inquisitiveness. Sufficient to the day is the trouble thereof.' He meant everyone had enough troubles and trials of their own without borrowing from others. And that included wanting to know more than she needed about other people.

She turned her attention back to Meggie. Despite her attempts to clean them up in the tiny town, they were both dusty and soiled, and smelled of coal smoke and sour milk. Not the way she would have wanted to arrive on a stranger's doorstep. She could only hope Meggie's new guardians cared nothing for such things and only for the well-being of their orphaned niece. Suddenly she wanted this meeting over with and had to remind herself to be patient. Like Pa would say, "Settle down, Pepper. You can't make the world turn faster."

They rounded a corner, ducked between two sharp

embankments crowned with a jagged row of rocks
and headed toward the buildings.

She strained forward, assessing everything. A
barn surrounded by rail fences with a horse in one
of the pens. Several low buildings on either side of
the alleyway running from the barn to the rambling
frame house that sat like the crowning jewel a little
apart. Smoke twisted from the rock chimney.

She squinted at the house as they drew closer,
anxious for a good look, wondering what sort of life
Meggie would be thrust into.

A roofed but wall-less lean-to covered the sides
of the house—a sort of veranda though it seemed to
come to an abrupt halt midway down one wall.

Even several hundred yards away she could see
an untidy assortment of things under the roof of the
lean-to. As if the barn wasn't big enough to accom-
modate the tools of ranching.

"We's here." The driver's announcement was
redundant as he pulled to a halt before the house.

"Could you please put my things on the porch?"

He yanked the two bags from the buggy and
deposited them. One contained her traveling things
and Meggie's few clothes. The other held most of
Lena's and a few of Mark's belongings. The bulk of
Mark's possessions had been claimed by his brother,
Andy, who also wanted to take Meggie but Lena had
been insistent that Meggie go to a married man.

"I don't want her raised by a bachelor. How would she learn to be a refined lady? No, promise me you'll take her to my brother. He sent for his bride six months ago. They'll be happily settled by now. My brother and I were always close. They'll take good care of my baby."

Jenny had gladly given her promise and would very shortly fulfill it.

She allowed the driver to help her from the buggy, carefully shifting Meggie from one arm to the other as she descended. The baby wakened and whimpered.

The man stood by his buggy. "I'll wait and see if anyone has letters to post."

Meggie hesitated. Why had no one come to the door or strode from one of the outbuildings? She'd glimpsed the shadow of a man in the barn. Seems someone should show a degree of curiosity if not neighborliness but apart from the creak of a gate blowing in the wind and the far-off cry of a hawk, there was no sound of welcome. "This is the right place?"

"The Lazy B. 'Spect all the men are out working but Paquette should be in the back. Want we should go that way?"

"Paquette?" What was that? But if it meant admission to this house, she'd follow the man most anywhere.

"She's the housekeeper. A Métis."

She'd heard of the part Indian, part French-Canadian people, many of them descended from the fur traders.

They left the baggage where the man put it and picked their way past overturned buckets and around a huddle of chairs.

They found the back door open. The driver stepped inside with complete confidence and Jenny followed hesitantly. In her world, one didn't walk into a house unbidden. This, however, was a strange, exciting new world. A thrill trickled through her lungs.

The enormous size of the room surprised her. A scarred wooden table with plank benches along each side and a chair at each end took up the area nearest the door. At the far end, cupboards and a stove— presided over by a little woman so bent and crippled Meggie wondered if she could walk. Her graying hair hung in twin braids down her back, tied with a length of leather. The frayed ends of each braid were black.

"Hullo, Paquette. The boss man about?" the man at her side called.

"I hear him soon ago. Out by de corrals, him. He ride away 'gain. I hear horsesteps. I help you? Me?"

Jenny edged past the driver. "My name is Jenny

Archibald. I need to speak to the Edwards. Could
you tell Mrs. Edwards I'm here?"

Bent as she was, the woman appeared to regard
Jenny from beneath her gray-streaked, black hair
with eyes so dark the pupils were indiscernible. "Be
no Missus Edwards." She gave a jerky sort of laugh
that seemed oddly full of both mirth and mockery.

"But—" Jenny fell back a step. "There must be."

"No, Ma'am, there is not." The deep voice behind
her jerked Jenny about so fast it hurt her eyes. She
blinked. It was the man from the train. Except—

She narrowed her eyes and looked at him more
closely. He looked like a wild cowboy now but with
the same dark intense eyes. Yes, it was the same
man.

She gathered her thoughts and chose the most
obvious one. "Mr. Edwards, I presume?"

"That would be so, though I prefer to be called
Burke. But tell me, why must I have a wife?" His
words were slow, his voice deadly calm.

She shivered at the way he spoke as if she had
insulted him and he was about to demand some sort
of retribution. Suddenly the strength drained out the
soles of her well-worn black leather boots. As her
knees turned soggy, she groped toward the table and
plunked down on a bench.

"Perhaps you better explain what it is you want."

He signaled to the woman. "Paquette, bring us coffee, please. Unless…" He silently questioned Jenny.

"Might I have tea?" she whispered.

"Tea, for the lady, Paquette."

"Yes, boss. Fer de lady. I get de tea."

Jenny pulled in a long, strengthening draft of air, hot from the stove and rolling with scents of many meals past and present. An explanation, he wanted, did he? Well, seems he had some explaining to do himself. Maybe she'd misunderstood. "No wife?"

"No wife now or ever."

"But—"

Mr. Edward's expression stopped any comment she'd been about to make. Lena said he had sent for his intended six months ago. They should have been married by now.

She reminded herself of all the times Ma had warned her to control her emotions, speak like a lady. *Mama, how would a lady speak and act in this situation?* Thoughts of Ma settled her and common sense replaced her shock. She'd deal with the facts one at a time.

"Mr. Edwards, I have come with some bad news."

His eyes narrowed and he sat down a few feet away, forcing her to shift sideways to look into his face.

Ignoring the thunderous warning in his face, not

even pausing to wonder what it meant, she rushed on. "I'm sorry to have to inform you your sister, Lena, and her husband, Mark, succumbed to the fever a few days ago. And I have brought your niece to you."

The man jolted like she'd stomped on his foot and she knew a certain satisfaction at surprising him as much as he'd done her. Her inappropriate feeling fled as quickly at it had come, replaced by sympathy. He'd lost his sister and brother-in-law. "I'm so sorry. Please accept my condolences."

And somehow he'd managed to lose the woman who was to be his wife. What had happened to her? Why didn't Lena know this? It sounded very suspicious and she glanced about as if the corners held secrets.

"They're gone? Both of them?" He swallowed hard and shifted his gaze to the little girl. "This is Meggie?"

Meggie whimpered at the sound of her name.

"She's hot and tired and missing her parents." The details regarding his lack of a wife could be sorted out later, after Meggie had been tended to. But what the baby needed most was a new mother figure.

There was no Mrs. Edwards. She tried to get her thoughts around the unwelcome information. Jenny glanced at the man in continuing disbelief.

His gaze held hers in the same steady probing look

that had trapped her on the train. She tried to free herself. Tried to think what she must do now.

Paquette set steaming cups at the table.

The driver sucked back black tea.

Jenny bent her head, ran her finger along the tiny handle.

This was not how things were to be.

Chapter Two

Burke stared at the young woman. Lena was dead? His baby sister and her husband? The only family he had? A sour taste like gall stung his throat. He'd cared for Lena after their parents died when he was sixteen and she fourteen. He'd found work, provided them a home, been her chaperone at outings. Only when she had Mark to care for her had he felt free to head west, full of plans for the future. He'd never considered Lena wouldn't always be there. He should have stayed and protected her. But shouldn't Mark have been doing that?

They were both gone. Taken by something no one could control but God. And God seemed not to care about the troubling affairs of individuals. No doubt He had his hands full running the world and taking care of the stars in space.

Burke had gotten his ranch. He'd planned to be

married by how, perhaps even have a new little Edwards boy or girl to look forward to.

That wasn't going to happen now. Suddenly he felt very alone.

He considered the fussing child. This baby was Meggie? He'd never seen her except for a likeness Lena had sent in a letter. He hadn't seen Lena and Mark since their marriage just before he headed west.

He choked back the thick bitterness clogging the back of his throat. Meggie was the only family he had left. A fierce protectiveness clawed at his gut. This child was now his. But what was he going to do with a little girl? If she'd been a boy...

The young woman coughed discreetly. "This changes everything. Lena was very clear that Meggie was to be raised by a mother and father. I'll take her back home and raise her myself. After I marry."

His fists clenched of their own accord. He uncurled them and planted his hands on his knees, deceptively calm while inside raged a storm a thousand times more fierce than the one he had endured only yesterday at Flora's side. The thought of losing Meggie about tore his heart out. And who was this stranger that she thought she had a say in it?

"I think we better start at the beginning. I'm Burke Edwards, Lena's brother and now Meggie's guardian. This is my home." He waved a hand to encompass

the room where they sat, suddenly aware of the inad-
equacies of his home. The leather straps he'd been
soaping tossed in the corner, the clutter of pots hung
on the wall because the cupboard he'd started to build
sat in the back of the barn, unfinished. The rest of
the house offered even less. The front room only a
thought in his head, the bedrooms, intended for a
family, used mostly for storage except for the one
Paquette occupied.

To her credit the woman before him revealed little
shock as she glanced about. "Pleased to meet you.
I'm Jenny Archibald." She held out a very tiny hand
clad in soft kid leather.

He spared her a closer look. She wore what he
expected was a fashionably appropriate but totally
impractical bonnet. Her traveling outfit was of fine
gray broadcloth although it now showed signs of her
trip. She was every inch a city girl though her eyes
blared with challenge.

"How did you know Lena?"

"We became friends when they moved to Center
City, Ohio."

"Ahh."

"Lena and Mark were very specific in their
instructions regarding their daughter."

Did he detect a hint of defiance in her voice? And
the sheen of tears in her eyes. No doubt she found
this whole ordeal most taxing. Well, he could relieve

her of her problems immediately. "No need for you to concern yourself further about my niece. I will assume responsibility for her here and now. You can return with Mr. Zach." He indicated the man she'd hired from the livery barn who watched the proceedings with avid curiosity. By the time he was back in town in fifteen minutes, everyone would know Burke's current situation. He drew in a breath that had to struggle past an angry tightness. Adding this to the speculation about Flora and Burke would provide enough fodder for many a delicious evening of head shaking and *tsking*.

Jenny drew herself tall and gave him a look fit to brand his forehead. "And how, may I ask, do you intend to care for a two-year-old child?"

"I'll manage."

Paquette mumbled something in French or perhaps Cree in the background.

"It isn't like I'm here alone."

Jenny's eyes flickered in disbelief and if he wasn't mistaken, amusement was the reason her eyes crinkled at the corners. "I suppose you intend to put her on a horse and teach her to hold the reins as you chase cows."

It was so close to what he figured he'd do that he lowered his eyes lest she see his acknowledgement. Meggie had the same golden brown hair and light brown eyes Lena had. "She's very much like her mother." The way his voice had grown soft revealed far too much of what he felt—loss and pain that twisted through him with the cruelty of an internal auger.

"She is." Jenny's voice softened too and trembled slightly. She cleared her throat. "I realize she's your niece. I'm sure you feel a sense of responsibility toward her, but be honest. You can't possibly hope to provide her with a proper home." She pushed to her feet, ignoring Meggie's wails. Perching the child on one hip she turned to Paquette. "Thank you for tea."

"Baby need food. Need loving. Need sleep, her." The two women considered each other silently, some unspoken message passing between them.

Burke watched, wondering about the way Paquette's eyes flashed from Meggie to him.

Jenny turned to Mr. Zach. "May I ride back to Buffalo Hollow with you?"

Zach scrambled from the table. "Certainly, ma'am."

Jenny took two steps toward the door, Meggie clutched to her side, before Burke realized what she had in mind.

He bolted to his feet. "Now hold on just one minute. I am this child's uncle and as her last living relative, I am most certainly her guardian. You can ride back to Buffalo Hollow with Zach and catch the next train back home but you are not taking Meggie with you." He reached for the little girl.

Meggie's eyes grew wide. Her mouth opened in a perfect O. She clung to Jenny's neck. For a moment, Burke struggled to extract the child from Jenny's arms. Jenny would not release her and Meggie fought him.

"Let her go," Burke ordered.

A fierce, angry look crossed Jenny's face and then it fled. She nodded and released her grasp.

Meggie screeched fit to stampede every cow within a hundred miles. She threw her head back, arched her little body and turned into a writhing bundle of resistance.

Burke almost dropped her in surprise. His ears hurt from the noise. But he had to prove he could handle this. "Meggie, I'm your Uncle Burke." He had to shout and even then he doubted Meggie heard a thing. She was every bit as hard to hold as an eight hundred pound steer as she reached for Jenny. Burke backed up so she couldn't touch the woman. But Meggie refused to come with him and hung suspended between the two.

Jenny watched, silently challenging him to admit defeat.

He would not. He turned his back on her and held the child so they were face to face. "Meggie, look at me."

But Meggie tossed her head side to side, still screaming, tears washing her face. He sat her on the table hoping that would calm her. It didn't and he struggled to keep her from throwing herself flat-out.

Paquette shuffled over. "Boss man not know babies. Boss man need help, no?"

Obviously he did. He nodded toward Paquette indicating she could help him.

She shook her head. "Paquette not strong no more. Paquette not look after baby." She waved toward Jenny. "Give baby to lady."

"No!" He shouted the word. Startled, Meggie gulped back a sob and stared at him, her eyes wide and filled with fear. It burned clear through that she should be afraid of him. But it was only because they were strangers. "I've lost everything, everyone. Meggie is all I have left." Seems God was prepared to allow him this much and he wasn't about to let it go.

At the sound of her name, Meggie again shrieked.

Paquette shook her head. "Boss man biting off big chunk of tough meat." She retreated to the stove.

Surely Meggie would soon run out of steam. But she showed no sign of relenting.

He flung a look over his shoulder.

Jenny and Zach stood at the doorway. Zach looked ready to fly away in a heartbeat. Jenny simply stood patiently, her arms crossed as if she knew he wouldn't be able to handle the child and waited for him to admit it.

At that moment he knew nothing in the world would induce him to let this child go. "She isn't going to settle so long as you're there. Please leave. Go back to town with Zach."

Meggie's wails did not let him forget how powerless he was to deal with her.

"Mr. Zach, you can go," Jenny said. "I'm not going to leave Meggie like this."

The man nodded and strode away.

Jenny knew her eyes flashed defiance. It was an attitude she'd tried hard to quell but Burke's behavior undid all her carefully fought gains. How dare he tell her to leave? As if she were to blame for the fact Meggie was crying. As well she should. She'd never seen this man before and he had rudely wrenched her from Jenny's grasp.

Being her uncle gave him no right.

As she boldly, defiantly met his startled look, she realized what she'd done. This was not what she'd planned. A few days. A week. Two if she pushed it, to allow Meggie time to get used to her new guardians, with a Mrs. Edwards taking over Meggie's care. Then Jenny would return home to her promises. Now what?

It wasn't like she had a lot of choice. She glanced around. A crippled old woman who mumbled and fiddled with things on the cupboard and made it clear as the air outside the door that she wasn't up to looking after a child. As if she needed to speak the words. Her first look had given Jenny the necessary information. Paquette was so crippled Jenny wondered if she could lift a pot of water which she did so right before Jenny's eyes. Barely. The woman must be in constant pain.

She shifted her attention back to Burke. He looked like he wanted to throw a brand on the baby.

She could hardly leave Meggie here under these circumstances.

"Where is your…fiancée?"

Paquette grumbled loudly but Jenny couldn't make out what she said.

Burke scowled. "She's gone. That's all you need to know."

Well, fine. He was entitled to his secrets, as was she.

Then the enormity of her situation hit her and she plunked to the hard bench. Here she was with a man who looked like he cared nothing what people thought and an old woman who—what would Ma and Pa think? What would they say? Pa had warned her to act wisely, speak carefully and live a life that gave people no cause to whisper about her. She knew her reputation was a precious thing and didn't intend to compromise it. She shivered. Not after her narrow escape.

Meggie thrust herself into Jenny's arms and Jenny held her close, finding comfort in the way the baby clung to her. She had a responsibility to this little one. But would everyone understand her choice?

She fired another look at Burke. "I intend to stay until suitable arrangements have been made for this child and she is settled." Her decision raised all sorts of quandaries. "Where do you...will I—?" Heat crawled up her neck and stung the tips of her ears. She couldn't even voice her concern. Where did he sleep? Where would she sleep?

Burke leaned back on the heels of his dusty cowboy boots and grinned. "Got yourself into a predicament, did you? Didn't check out the situation before you made your bold decision?"

Bold. The word clawed through her mind. How often had Pa said she was too bold? How often had Ma said it would get her into trouble?

Boots thudded on the wooden floor outside and Mr. Zach appeared, carrying her luggage. "Thought I'd carry your bags inside."

"Not too late to change your mind and go back with Zach."

Burke's voice was low, insistent, as if he not only

thought she should do so, but felt an urgency she should.

Meggie in her arms, she pushed to her feet and faced him knowing her determination blared across her face. "If I can take Meggie."

"'Fraid I can't let you do that."

Slowly she nodded. "Then I'm afraid I must stay with her until you get married."

Ignoring Burke's sputter of protest, she thanked Mr. Zach, who hesitated then slowly retreated. As she listened to the buggy rattle from the yard she knew she was irrevocably committed to this decision.

She stared hard at Burke, each of them taking stock of the other's reserve of stubbornness. She narrowed her eyes, hoped he would see she would not back down. Not now. Not ever. Not until arrangements were up to what Lena would expect.

The look he gave her might have made her shiver if she had been the quiet, refined lady her parents hoped for instead of one who acted first, thought later, afraid of nothing and no one. She remembered Ma's admonition to moderate her boldness and lowered her gaze. "I hope we can arrange a suitable living arrangement."

Burke snorted. "And what do you intend to do if we can't? Shouldn't you have thought of that before you sent Zach away?" He sighed. "It's too late to ride with him but I'll take you back."

"Why are you so determined to get rid of me?"

"Because you don't belong. Better you accept it right now before you get in over your head."

Little did he know that she was already in that situation, but it would not cause her to abandon Meggie whose warm arms clung around Jenny's neck, her face buried against Jenny's shoulder.

"It's not too late to change your mind."

"I'll let you know when I'm ready to leave. But I can assure you it won't be until I'm satisfied Meggie will be properly taken care of."

His gaze darkened. "I don't think that's your call to make."

"I disagree. Lena and Mark trusted me with seeing Meggie properly settled. I intend to do just that. Now—" she glanced about "—if you would be kind enough to show me where we might clean up."

He didn't move a muscle or give any indication he would help in any way.

Jenny shot a glance toward Paquette who met her gaze with what Jenny could only take as a mixture of pity and compassion.

"Boss, she and baby use room next mine. It be big 'nough."

Burke groaned. "This is a mistake we'll all live to regret."

Jenny didn't know if he addressed her or Paquette but she understood her decision to stay was the mistake he referred to, and it undid all her efforts at being reserved. "I fail to see why you should view this as a disaster in the making. I simply have a job to do—see Meggie is settled." She refrained from adding she would insist on several other changes, too—but a glance around revealed a hundred things that would be dangerous to a toddler. And it didn't require more than a fleeting acquaintance with the setup to realize there was no one in the present company who could care for Meggie. Until she solved that problem she would be staying. "I think if we all cooperate things should go swimmingly."

He looked at the roof as if hoping for divine help.

Exactly what she needed. *My Father in heaven, guide me and protect me as I help Meggie settle in. Help me be wise and cautious.*

"Paquette, show her the room." He headed for the door then paused. "Miss Archibald, I will say it again. This is no place for a woman. You might do well to heed my warning."

Before he could escape, Jenny spoke. "I'll leave when I deem it's appropriate but I won't be run off. I won't be scared off. So don't even try."

He turned slowly, his expression full of pity. "Don't flatter yourself that I'd bother. You'll find plenty of challenges without my interference."

What on earth did he mean? A trembling worm of

warning skittered across her neck. Was there some sort of danger she should be aware of? But he was gone before she could ask. That left Paquette as her only source of information. "What was he talking about? Is there something I should know?"

Paquette grinned, her black eyes snapping. "Boss be…" She fluttered her hands as if to indicate the man was unstable.

The trembling in Jenny's neck developed talons. Was the man dangerous? She'd heard tales of men losing their minds out in the vast empty prairie. Why, Pa had saved a newspaper story just to show her, warn her. "You need to be on your guard, Pepper. Strange things happen out there and you'll be on your own." For proof he'd allowed her to read the story of a bachelor who had gone out of his head from the loneliness and ran out into the cold clad only in his union suit, firing his rifle into the air. The report said it was a miracle no one had been shot.

"He's not given to doing strange things, is he?" She needed answers, needed to know what to expect so she could be ready.

Paquette looked surprised then chortled. "He not the crazy one."

Somehow Jenny found that less than assuring. "Who is?"

The older woman shook her head. "Lots people

crazy. Lots people. Now come. I show you de room."

Jenny wanted more information. Who was crazy? Were they a threat to her? Or more importantly, Meggie? Then she followed Paquette into a room and her questions were forgotten.

"Need cleaning, it."

Jenny almost laughed at Paquette's understated words. From what she could see the room served as a catchall for both farm and home. Bits of wood were scattered on one side along with hammer, saw and nails. As if a building project had come to a halt at that very spot. As obviously it had. The walls were unfinished uprights. The window only roughly framed. It looked like the abandoned building materials had served as a magnet to other forgotten items— an overcoat, foot warmers, a bundle of canvas….

She shuddered. She and Meggie were expected to sleep here?

"Boss man sleep bunkhouse. Wit de men, him. For long time now. Since—" She didn't finish.

Another secret. "Since when, Paquette?"

Paquette shook her head and backed from the room. "You be fixing room, no?"

Jenny understood she would be getting no answers from Paquette. All she could do was keep her eyes open and be alert to anything out of the ordinary. In the meantime…

She stared at the room. Only one way to get it ready for habitation…start hauling out stuff. She cleared a spot for Meggie in the center of the bed, retrieved her bags and found a little blanket for the baby to sit on. She pulled out the little rag doll Lena had so lovingly stitched and settled Meggie to play.

As she worked, words raced through her head— crazy, warning, mistake. There were far too many unanswered questions for her to feel safe. She heard the sound of horse hooves and picked her way across the room to the window in time to see Burke ride away, his well-worn cowboy hat pushed low on his head, leaning forward as if anxious to be away from this place. She shivered. Should she be afraid of him?

He turned, saw her at the window. His gaze drilled into her, dark, powerful, full of—

She jerked back and pressed her palm to her throat.

Promise? Hope? Or was it despair? Warning?

Was she seeing things she wanted to or things that were real?

In a flash she thought of the way he watched her on the train. Had he been kind or something sinister? No. He'd been kind and polite. Her imagination was simply getting out of control. He'd defended her before the others in the train. He'd helped her with her bags.

And he'd warned her not once but twice that she didn't belong here.

Why? What lay behind his warning? Kindness or something else? What secret lay behind his not being married?

Sufficient to the day is the trouble thereof.

Pa's oft-spoke words released her tensions and she laughed. None of those things mattered. She had a task to do and she would do it. She would keep her promise to Lena and Mark.

Meggie had fallen asleep, the rag doll clutched in one hand.

While she slept, Jenny quickly changed into a dark skirt and a wrinkled shirtwaist. It could do with ironing but at least it was clean and considerably cooler than her traveling outfit. Then she surveyed the room. There was nothing she enjoyed more than a task of significance and this was a big one. She tackled the job with vigor, singing softly as she worked.

Burke rode for half an hour, a leisurely, enjoy-the-quiet type ride. Out here he found peace and solitude—something he feared he would not find at home in the future.

He reached the spring Mac had expressed concern about, took his shovel and attacked it, tossing out heaps of dirt. The work did its job—releasing the tension that started at the first sight of Jenny in his house, and built steadily throughout her announcement that Lena and Mark had died until it peaked when she informed him she would stay. He should have insisted she leave. Before this country sent her screaming into the distance.

He paused to suck in air. Lena was dead. Her husband, too. He let sorrow drench his pores, let it ease out in the sweaty drops beading his skin. He would miss her.

The Lord giveth and the Lord taketh away.

He would not finish the sentence...*blessed be the name of the Lord*. The taking held no blessing in his opinion. Only regret and sorrow. Deep sorrow.

He returned to digging out the hole until water broke loose and flowed freely into the shallow pit he'd fashioned last year. At the scent and sound of water, a nearby cow bellowed and headed toward him. The call echoed across the short grass and was picked up and passed along by other cows until he could see them running like a living, shrinking circle.

The first cow saw him and balked. A human on foot made her nervous.

He obligingly swung into the saddle.

The cow tossed her head and raced onward, her calf skipping at her side.

The herd neared. As they crowded in for water, he smiled. A man could forget his troubles out here.

And just like cows heading for water his thoughts headed for home. What was he going to do about Jenny? She didn't belong out in this country. But he couldn't seem to persuade her otherwise. And until he did, he was stuck with her.

How could he best prove to her he didn't need her?

He thought of little Meggie crying and struggling in his arms and amended his question—he didn't need her for long.

He considered his options. First, he didn't want any pretty young woman languishing out here in order to care for Meggie. He would manage her care. All he had to do was give her a few days to get used to him and then he would simply take her with him as he worked. She'd grow up as his sidekick.

Someone to share his life with. The idea gave him a jolt of pleasure.

Carefully, he laid out his plan. A few days for her to get to know him, and then they'd ride and work together.

And Jenny could return to her safe home back east. Before it was too late.

That settled, he reined around and headed back to the ranch. Paquette would wonder at him returning before suppertime but he figured the sooner he got working on his plan, the sooner it would be fulfilled.

A few minutes later, he strode toward the house, trying to think how he should start getting to know Meggie. Only two years old. No doubt shy. Certainly frightened. Like a barn kitten seeing a human up close for the first time. He'd tame Meggie the same way…slow, patient and with…he laughed. Doubted she would like milk straight from the cow in a warm stream. What did a child like? Perhaps Paquette would know.

He slipped inside. The kitchen was empty but sounds came from the far side of the house. He followed the voices around the house and stopped short at what he saw.

Jenny stood before a stack of boards and blankets, boots and saws all in a heap fifty feet from the house. She'd taken off the ridiculously impractical thing she wore on her arrival and wore an ordinary shirt and skirt. Not that he thought it changed who she really was.

She spoke to Paquette. "I'm sure it can be arranged for someone to haul this stuff away where it will pose no threat to a small child."

Paquette stood on the veranda shaking her head and making disapproving noises. "Boss not like stuff throw out like dis."

"Meggie and I can't sleep in the midst of debris and dirt. She's a baby. She needs a safe, clean environment."

Burke sighed and filled in the other things Jenny no doubt figured Meggie needed—things like neighbors, church, town activities, pretty clothes. He'd heard it all. Tried to convince Flora those things weren't necessary but it was the land itself that defeated him. Flora thought the prairies desolate; the wind haunting. She swore they would drive her mad.

She was right in the end.

But he would teach Meggie to be different.

He could only do it without some city gal filling her mind with frivolities.

He cleared his throat to announce his presence.

"I finish de supper," Paquette said and shuffled indoors.

Jenny dusted her hands. "I'm cleaning out the room you've allotted me."

"So I see. Is all this necessary?"

She smiled. "I guess only you could say. But necessary or not, it won't be sharing my quarters."

He knew from the way her eyes flashed that she had purposely misunderstood him. He meant was it necessary to move everything out to the middle of the yard. But he let it pass. "Where's Meggie?"

"Sleeping. I better check on her." She would have slipped past him except he moved to block her path.

"I think you better accept that we have different agendas here."

Her eyebrows headed for the sky. "Really? I thought we both had Meggie's best interests in mind. Her health and safety and happiness. Am I mistaken in thinking so?"

Her quiet challenge edged through his arguments and completely disarmed him. "On Meggie's behalf, we are agreed. But you won't be staying any longer than it takes for me and Meggie to make friends."

Her eyes clear as the sky above, she stared at him. "I'll leave when I decide everything is as it ought to be for Meggie." She swung away then turned back. "Unless you figure to have me bodily removed."

The idea tickled his insides. Somehow he suspected it would require three strong men and a long length of sturdy rope. His amusement trickled into his eyes. He felt them crinkle. Then it caught his mouth and filled his throat and he laughed. "Let's hope it doesn't come to that."

She blinked at his laughter then her stubbornness seemed to melt away. "I do tend to get all bristly, don't I? I'm here to see Meggie is settled. We should be able to tolerate each other long enough to accomplish that." And she marched away.

He scrubbed his chin with one finger. Tolerate her? Now why should she think that? But perhaps she'd been thinking she would tolerate him. Ah well. He had nothing to offer a fine lady. He knew it. His life consisted of the vast lonely prairie and the company of cows and cowboys. He'd teach Meggie to appreciate it all but he had no such misconceptions regarding any young woman. He'd put up with her tolerance only as long as he needed.

Mac and Dug rode to the bunkhouse and Burke sauntered over to see how things were.

"Good to have you back, boss."

"Good to be back." He better warn them before they stomped into the house for supper. "There's company up at the house."

"Yeah?"

He could almost feel their ears perk up with interest. The last time he'd had company...no point in thinking about that. It was history. A lesson well learned for them all.

Lucky joined them. Burke felt their cautious curiosity but it was Mac who broke the barrier of silence. "Flora?" His voice was courteous, revealing nothing though Burke knew they likely all hoped to never put up with her dramatics again.

"Flora won't be back. Ever."

A silent sigh filled the air.

"She's still in the—"

Burke nodded. "Her parents are with her. They told me not to come again. Blamed me for how she is." No more than he blamed himself. He shouldn't have pushed her, shouldn't have asked so much from her.

The four men turned and stared at the house.

Burke realized he still hadn't provided them with the necessary information. "My niece is here. Meggie. She's only two."

He chuckled at the way all heads turned and surprised eyes stared at him.

Dug swallowed hard, his long thin neck working all the way down. "A little gal?"

Mac, ever practical and blunt said, "Why?"

"My sister and her husband died. I'm now Meggie's guardian."

"Sorry, boss," the three mumbled in unison.

He joined them in staring toward the house. "A young woman brought her out."

The men shuffled but no one spoke, as if waiting for Burke to say more.

"Name's Jenny and she's staying to get Meggie settled in."

Dug took a straw from his pocket and picked at his teeth. Mac crossed his arms and stared at the house, his expression dour. Burke didn't bother glancing at Lucky. He felt again their reluctance to voice their concerns about another young woman visiting the ranch.

"She won't be here long."

A couple of grunts.

"She hauled all the junk out of the second bedroom and piled it in the middle of the yard on the other side of the house."

Cautious nods.

"Guess we best haul it away." He strode across the yard, the men in his wake. They rounded the corner and viewed the pile of junk.

"Boss, all this was in a bedroom?"

"Yup."

"What was ya thinking?"

He shrugged. "Had no need of another bedroom. Paquette only needs one." He didn't say the bedroom had been meant for him and Flora. Suddenly the men figured it out and shut up. Except Mac.

"You say this young woman hauled all this out by herself?"

"I came from cleaning out the spring and found it here."

The men grabbed armloads. "Where you want it?" Dug asked.

"I don't know. In the barn. Beside the barn. Wherever you think it should be."

Lucky paused at Burke's side, his arms loaded with lengths of lumber. "Must be a right spunky gal to drag this all out by herself."

Spunky? Huh. He didn't know about that. "All I seen was her stubbornness."

Mac chuckled softly. "A bird of a different feather maybe."

The men seemed cheered by that thought as they moved the pile of stuff.

Burke didn't care what sort of feathers she wore so long as she nested them far away from here. As soon as possible.

Chapter Three

Jenny held Meggie's hand and led her to the kitchen. Her job at the present was to get Meggie settled and that included introducing her to the house and its occupants.

"Meggie, say hello to Mrs. Paquette."

"It be only Paquette." The woman bent forward even more until she was almost eyeball to eyeball with Meggie. The beaded necklace she wore hung within easy grasp. "Pretty baby." She patted Meggie's head.

Meggie chuckled and reached for the necklace.

"Don't touch, Meggie," Jenny warned.

"Baby not hurt it." Paquette slipped the necklace over her head and hung it around Meggie's neck. "You play with."

"Paquette, are you sure? She might break it or lose it."

"Not break. Leather string. Not lose. Too big."

"Thank you. Meggie, tell the lady thank you."

Meggie looked up from patting the beads. "Pretty. Thank you for pretty."

Paquette seemed satisfied and turned back to her chores.

"What can I do to help?"

The woman grew very still, her back to Jenny. "I not need help. I be strong as bear."

Jenny immediately realized the woman felt challenged, as if Jenny had suggested she couldn't manage. "I'm sure you do very well but I can't sit around and watch you work. I intend to make myself useful while I'm here."

Paquette turned slowly and studied Jenny with bottomless eyes. Finally she nodded. "Set de table."

"Great. How many?"

"Burke and three men. Me."

She hadn't included Jenny and Meggie. Was it intentional? Was she not going to be allowed to eat with the others? That wasn't going to work. Not if Meggie were to feel at home with whomever lived here. Her mind made up, she nodded. "With myself and Meggie that would be seven places."

She held Paquette's startled gaze, refusing to back down. Finally the older woman nodded. "Seven." And turned back to the big pots on the stove.

Jenny found the plates and silverware. She found

battered tin cups and put them on. "Shall I fill a jug with water?"

"Water at pump."

Jenny already had noticed the pump at one end of the cupboard. Much more convenient than having to run outside for water. She found a large enamel jug. As she pumped the water, she looked out the window.

Burke stood at a low building with three men at his side. They all stared toward the house as if waiting for something. Burke reached up and pushed his hat back. The sun hit his face, making each feature sharp. Suddenly he grinned, his gaze still aimed at the house. Her heart skittered in alarm. Did he see her? She backed away. But if he did, he wouldn't likely smile. He had been less than welcoming. And she had been even less compliant. She had forgotten her upbringing. *Father God, forgive me for being so quick to speak my mind. Help me cause no offense.*

She vowed she would not react to any further comments from Burke about how soon she would leave and how glad he would be for that time.

The jug was full. As she lifted it Burke and the men trooped across the yard and past the house. A few minutes later they returned, all with their arms full of the things she'd hauled from the bedroom. She chuckled.

Paquette looked out the window to see what amused her. "Boss not like moving stuff."

Jenny shrugged. What could he do about it? "What else does the boss not like?"

Paquette turned as fast as her crippled body allowed and her mouth worked as she stared at Jenny.

What on earth? It was a simple enough question meant only to help Jenny know how to avoid any upsets. Why did the woman look so sad? Or was it anger?

Paquette ducked away. "Boss not like be hurt."

"Ahh." So it was probably both sadness and anger. "And has he been hurt somehow?"

"He not say. I not say."

That was extremely unhelpful but Jenny knew Paquette would say no more. She couldn't help admiring the woman for not dipping into gossip or sharing secrets. A most honorable trait.

Paquette checked the pots again. "You ring for men."

"Sure. How?"

"Out de door."

Jenny took that to mean the bell hung outside the door. "Come on Meggie, want to help me ring the bell?"

"Me help."

Hand in hand they went outside. Jenny looked

around for a bell. Saw none. She looked again. Saw
a metal rod hanging from the rafters. Another piece
of rod hung from a nail nearby. This must be the
bell. She banged the rods together creating a great
clatter.

"Me help."

She gave the metal bar to Meggie and held her up
to bang the bell. Meggie laughed. "Me do more." She
banged and banged, giggling with each crash. Then
she handed the rod to Jenny. "You do again."

Jenny batted at the rod, the racket vastly satisfying. A great way to deal with frustration and she hit
the swinging bar as hard as she could. It went flying.
She followed its journey and gulped as it landed at
the tip of a pair of boots.

Jenny was almost certain she had seen that particular set of footwear already today. Knew they
belonged to a man who wasn't terribly glad to have
her here. This would not make him any more glad.
Slowly she raised her gaze until it connected with a
pair of dark eyes. "Whoops. Guess I got a little too
vigorous."

"Either there's a fire or the meal is about to dry
up and blow away."

She swallowed hard.

The men she'd seen earlier flanked Burke. She
couldn't look at any of them as embarrassment jour-
neyed up her neck and seared its way across her

cheeks. She shifted Meggie closer, feeling the child's wariness of all these strangers.

"Supper's ready." She fled indoors.

Paquette chuckled. "Big racket. Bring de man fast. No?"

"Yes." Next time she would be more circumspect, more controlled. But a grin tugged at her mouth. It had been fun and maybe next time she'd ring it every bit as hard.

The men had paused at the washstand outside the door and now trooped in and began to take places at the table. Suddenly they saw the number was off and paused, glancing around for someone to direct them.

Jenny hung back, Meggie still in her arms. It wasn't her place to say where they should sit but all eyes darted at her. If she wasn't mistaken they all held a bit of nervous wariness. "Please, just go ahead as you always would."

Paquette placed the heaping bowls on the table. "You be sit at end?" She indicated one of the chairs. The other chair stood at the far end and Burke stood at it like it was his customary place.

Why the sudden cautiousness? Was there a secret order or something? A place she could choose that would usurp some subtle hierarchy? One way to find out. "Where do you usually sit?" She directed her question at Paquette.

Paquette didn't answer but her gaze sought out the chair.

"You take the chair. I'll sit wherever is convenient."

"Sit," Burke ordered.

A general shuffle followed. Jenny hung back until the men sorted themselves out. The only empty places were next to Burke. She would have chosen to be closer to Paquette but the die was cast and she sat. Meggie refused to leave her lap so Jenny held her.

"Jenny," Burke said, "Let me introduce my men." He turned to his right. "Dug—

A man who appeared to be in his early twenties, as lean as a twist of rope, but with a friendly enough expression, grinned at her.

"Lucky—"

The man she'd glimpsed in the barn. Short, stocky and with a wide grin that made Jenny feel more welcome than she had since she landed on the ground in front of the house.

"Welcome, Miss Jenny," Lucky said.

Burke's gaze shifted across the table to the man at Jenny's left. "And Mac."

The man had red hair and a red beard and even though he smiled at her, he looked like he'd better fit a frown.

"Pleased to meet all of you and I look forward to getting to know you better during my visit."

If she wasn't mistaken they all shot wary looks at Burke. She wondered if he had told them she wouldn't be staying long.

"Eat," Paquette said. "Before de fat form."

Hands reached for the bowls.

Jenny cleared her throat. "Shouldn't someone say grace?"

The hands jerked back and disappeared under the table. A startled silence filled the room.

Jenny met Burke's eyes. "Lena would want Meggie raised in a Christian home."

Burke's eyes were hard and unyielding. "I ain't much for praying."

Wasn't he a Christian man? Lena certainly thought so. Or was it just discomfort at praying aloud? She waited. The men waited. The room pulsed with waiting.

Burke looked about the table. "Anyone else willing?"

The men mumbled. Only words Jenny made out indicated they thought the boss should do it.

Finally Dug cleared his throat. "Want me to do it?"

"Please." Burke sounded like he'd been saved some dreadful disaster.

They all bowed their heads. Paquette crossed herself.

Dug sucked in air. "We thank you, Father, for this

food. And pray you'll bless it to our good. Help us live your name to praise, in all we do through all our days. Amen." He gasped as he finished the words in a rush.

Mac cleared his throat.

"Eat," Paquette again ordered and the men dug in with haste as if they had to make up for lost time.

Meggie watched them for a moment, silently measuring and assessing.

"Meg, how about some food?" It had been ages since they'd had a good hot meal and the aromas coming from the pot roast and rich gravy made Jenny want to imitate the men in attacking her food. But she had Meggie to think about.

Meggie opened her mouth and waited for Jenny to feed her. She'd abandoned feeding herself after her parents died. Jenny understood it was only her way of coping—going backward a little to a safer, kinder time in her life.

No one spoke as they focused their attention on the food.

Finally Mac swiped his plate clean with a slice of bread and leaned back. Paquette placed a pot of coffee in the middle of the table and he poured himself a mug full.

"Hauled out all that stuff by yourself, did ya?"

Jenny realized he meant the junk from the bedroom. "I did."

"Not a nice job."

"Wasn't bad."

"Must have been pretty dirty."

"I sneezed a time or two." The others filled coffee cups and leaned back. For some reason they seemed mighty interested in this conversation. "Stomped a few spiders but nothing much."

Lucky chuckled. "See any big spiders." He held his hands out to indicate one about six inches across.

As a greenhorn Jenny knew she was open season for teasing but she wasn't falling for that one. She decided to turn the tables. "Phew. One that big is nothing." She held out her hands to the size Lucky indicated. Slowly she widened the distance between her hands until they were twelve inches apart. "There was one behind the stack of lumber that came at me with a piece of wood. But I fixed him."

All eyes were on her now. She glanced at Burke, saw his guarded expression. His eyes seemed to grab her and invite her to follow him into exciting adventures. She jerked her gaze away. She was being fanciful. Only place he wanted her was out of here.

"How'd you fix him?" Dug asked.

She glanced around the table, delaying the moment. When she felt everyone waiting for her answer she quirked an eyebrow in a dismissive, doesn't matter way. "I trapped him in a boot. Tied it shut. Put it on the veranda with its mate. Guess you all better be checking your footwear before you put it on."

The men stared. Burke laughed first. "She gotcha."

Startled laughter came from the others and Paquette cackled.

Jenny allowed herself a glance toward Burke. The skin at the corners of his eyes crinkled. His eyes weren't black as she'd first thought but dark brown and full of warm mirth. She couldn't pull away. Couldn't break the moment as they grinned at each other, something silent and sweet passing between them.

"I think she got *you*, boss," Mac murmured.

The laughter had ended. How long had they been staring into each other's eyes? Jenny jerked her gaze away and fussed with Meggie, who worked on a crust of bread.

Burke pushed from the table. "I got things to do."

The men all bolted to their feet and followed him from the room.

"I'll help clean up," Jenny offered as she rose from the table.

"It not for lady," Paquette protested.

"I'm not here to be pampered." She carried dishes to the cupboard and tackled washing them. Work was a good way to control her wayward thoughts.

As she worked she had but to lift her head to see Burke outside doing something at the corrals, Lucky at his side. Burke moved with a sureness revealing his strength and confidence.

A man who belonged in this new challenging land.

A man who drew some deep longing from a secret place behind her heart.

She jerked her thoughts to a standstill.

She'd listened to those siren voices before—adventure, excitement. It had led to disaster.

She pulled her gaze away.

Father God, help me be wise. Help me heed the counsel of my parents.

She washed the last dish, wiped the table clean. "I think I'll take Meggie out for a walk before bedtime. She needs fresh air and exercise."

She took Meggie's hand and together they went outdoors. She let Meg run the length of the veranda, smiling at the fun the child got from her shoes echoing on the wooden floor. When Meggie climbed down the three steps to the ground, Jenny followed. They wandered down the path toward the open field. The land rose almost imperceptibly but enough that suddenly the countryside lay before her like a great huge blanket. The sun dipped low in the west casting shadows across the land, filling it with dips and hollows. The light caught higher objects almost lifting them from the ground. The land went on and on. Amazing. Awesome.

Jenny lifted her arms to the sky.

She could almost touch the clouds. Float on them across the endless sky.

"Oh, Pa," she whispered. "If you could see this. Feel what I feel, you'd understand the restlessness of my soul." She didn't want to be confined within four walls, constrained by the bounds of town life.

But she would honor her parents. She lowered her arms and crossed them over her chest.

She would keep her word and return.

Surely, once she was back she would forget this moment.

She knew she never would. In fact, she stared at the vast prairie for a long time. She didn't want to forget. She wanted to brand it forever on her brain, a secret place she could visit in the future and find again, this wonderful sense of freedom.

Burke watched Jenny and Meggie head past the corrals. His arms tingled with apprehension. How would she react when she saw how empty the prairie was around her?

At his side, Lucky watched, too. "She's different."

Burke knew what Lucky meant—Jenny was different than Flora.

Lucky went on as if Burke had asked him to explain. "She's got a sense of humor, for one thing. And she sat with us like she didn't think she was better."

Flora had made it clear she would not share the table with servants. She'd wanted Burke to join her at eating separately, expecting Paquette to wait on them.

Burke had refused. It was only a small thing. He should have found a way to compromise. Perhaps it would have made a difference. He watched Jenny as she reached the end of the path and drew to a halt.

In the end it was the emptiness of the land that did in Flora. As it did so many. Why, just a few months ago the marshal had taken away Stan Jones to the north of here and Mr. Abernathy had packed up and gone back east because his wife couldn't take it anymore. Burke had heard Mrs. Abernathy now had a personal nurse to care for her.

Jenny raised her arms over her head. What was she doing? Trying to hold the emptiness at bay?

Lucky watched, too. "Is she laughing?"

Burke threw down the hammer he held and headed after her. If he didn't need her to help Meggie settle he would send her back to town first thing in the morning. Before her laughter took on a shrill note.

He had gone but twenty feet when she turned and

headed back toward the house. A smile wreathed her face. She looked positively happy—excited even.

Burke shifted direction and returned to the fence he'd been repairing with Lucky's help.

Lucky continued to stare at Jenny. "She's different, I tell ya."

Burke wouldn't watch her but he couldn't stop himself from glancing up from pounding a nail. She walked with a carefree swing. Her face glowed as she glanced skyward. Her laughter rang out as Meggie said something. From his first glance he'd been attracted. But nothing had changed—not the land and not him. "She's only been here a few hours and she isn't staying more than a few days. No need for her to concern herself with anything but Meggie." No need for her to think about what life was like out here, how living here day after day would feel.

"Boss, not all women are like Flora." Lucky made his soft comment then grabbed the other end of the plank and drove in a spike, making conversation impossible.

Burke stuffed back his response. It didn't matter whether Jenny was different or not. He wasn't about to repeat his hard-learned lesson.

Jenny and Meggie went inside and a crackling tension he'd been unaware of—or maybe just unwilling to admit—eased off.

He should ride out into the prairie until his

thoughts settled into acceptance of the reality of his life, but he lingered in the yard listening to the sounds coming from the open windows of the house.

Jenny must have put Meggie to bed. He heard the baby fussing then Jenny singing a lullaby. The notes caught his memories and teased them forward. He remembered his mother holding Lena and rocking her to the same tune. He hadn't thought of his mother in a long time. Not since he'd moved out west.

Now Lena and Mark were dead of a fever and he was guardian to their child. It was a repeat of when he became Lena's guardian.

They had done well together.

Only Meggie was so much younger.

Jenny's singing grew softer.

He strained toward the sound. It had stopped. Meggie must have fallen asleep. He drew in a relieved breath. Must be hard on such a little one to lose her parents and all.

But once she settled in, he would teach her how to have fun, how to enjoy the wild land. Satisfied, he headed for the barn.

A wrenching sob stopped him in his tracks. Meggie again. Poor child sounded heartbroken. No doubt she was.

Burke longed to be able to comfort his niece. Knew she wouldn't accept any offer from him. Jenny's soft, soothing tones underlay Meggie's cries and the child quieted again.

His heart flooded with gratitude to Jenny for comforting Meggie when he was powerless to do so.

He thought again of the way she'd flung her arms skyward, the brightness of her smile as she returned from her walk. He smiled remembering the spider joke she'd told the men. And how she'd sat at the table with everyone. Pictures of her calmness on the train brought again the flicker of admiration and interest he'd felt at the time.

He snorted. He would not be mistaking gratitude for attraction.

There were things he could do to keep himself busy in the barn and he headed that direction. As he checked harnesses and cleaned out a pen, he strained to catch any sounds from the house. No more crying. A relief. No more singing. Too bad—no, he was not disappointed.

The interior of the barn grew dark and he headed out into the dusk.

Against the darkening sky, at the end of the path, Jenny stood outlined, standing in the same spot where she'd been when he watched her with her arms raised.

From deep inside him a strident voice called, demanding acknowledgement. Something about this woman pulled at his heart, made him want things that were at cross-purposes with his intentions.

Drawn by a silent, invisible cord, he sauntered over to stand at her side. "Mighty lonely place."

"Listen."

He did so. "It's silent."

"No. It's full of whispers. I hear the breeze tickling the grass. It almost sings. And way off a bird is calling good night."

He listened, hearing tiny sounds he'd grown used to until he no longer heard them. The sky faded to gray. Pink hovered at the horizon.

"It's so pretty."

A mournful wail came from one side.

She turned toward the sound. "What's that?"

An answering howl came from another spot and a sharp yapping sound from another.

"Coyotes." He waited for her to shiver and head back to safety.

"They're singing." She sounded pleased rather than scared.

Flora had fled to the protection of the house, shivering and frightened. "Wild animals. This place is so uncivilized."

Seems Lucky was right. Jenny was different.

Not that it changed a thing. This country was hard enough for a man, not at all suitable for a woman.

They stood watching the last light fade, listening to the coyotes sing and the prairie whisper.

Unwilling to break the spell of contentment, he didn't speak though a thousand words flitted across his mind, questions about who she was, what her dreams were.

Finally she sighed. "I guess I better get back and make sure Meggie is okay."

She headed for the house and he fell in at her side.

Meggie. A topic he could safely mention. "It took her a long time to settle."

"Poor little girl. She's lost everything."

"She still has me." And you, until you leave.

"I'm sorry. I meant everything familiar."

He'd been too quick to take offense but wasn't sure how to correct it without drawing undue attention to the fact. "She'll soon settle in and feel at home here." Why did the idea not feel as good as it should?

"I expect so."

They'd reached the veranda and paused. "Good night," she said.

A lamp sat on the kitchen table and sent a golden glow through the window putting Jenny's face into a shadow.

He told himself he wasn't disappointed he couldn't see her expression as they parted ways.

He strode to the bunkhouse and headed for the

bed he'd claimed as his own six months ago when he'd convinced Flora to visit the ranch. He'd been so sure she would learn to love the place as he had even though she had insisted on staying in town for weeks.

He'd been wrong.

Jenny enjoyed the coyotes singing.

"Seen you out walking with Miss Jenny," Dug called. "Pretty gal."

"She ain't staying," Burke growled. He didn't want her to. Wouldn't ask her to consider it.

He turned on his side, giving the men a good view of his back, indicating this topic of conversation was over. He felt their watchful stillness then rustling as they settled themselves at something else.

If only his thoughts would obey as quickly but they kept painting pictures on the inside of his eyelids— Jenny walking and laughing with Meggie, Jenny at the table telling a joke. Jenny reaching for the sky.

He opened his eyes so he couldn't see the pictures, but then sounds filled his thoughts.

Jenny singing to Meggie. Jenny laughing. Jenny whispering at the magic of the prairie evening song.

He groaned silently.

How long would it take for Meggie to settle in?

It couldn't be too soon for his peace of mind. The sooner Jenny left, the better.

Chapter Four

Jenny lay on her bed fighting her thoughts. It was wrong to think of Burke as she did. After all, she was all but promised to another man. She'd given her word to her parents. Yet here she lay with every word Burke had said, every gesture he'd made playing over and over in her mind. But even those memories weren't as condemning as her wayward reactions.

She'd almost grabbed his hand in excitement when she heard the coyotes howl—a mournful sound that made her want to sing along. If Burke hadn't been at her side she might have tried imitating them.

Besides being wrong, her thoughts were so futile. He made it clear she wasn't welcome here. And there was still the mystery of the missing fiancée. What happened to her? He said he'd never marry but perhaps he was only angry with the woman. A lover's quarrel.

She focused on that thought until her wayward imaginations came into order.

Father God, be Thou my hiding place. Keep me safe from my impetuous nature.

Finally she fell asleep.

Twice during the night, Meggie wakened and Jenny sang to settle her.

Next morning, she rose with her resolve returned. She had a task to complete. Today she would start doing things necessary to get Meggie ready for her to leave.

She knelt at the bedside, careful not to disturb Meggie who still slept. *Father God, I need Your guidance today. Put a watch before my mouth so I speak only kind words. Show me the things I need to change for Meggie's sake. Most of all enable me to guard my heart so I don't think and feel foolish, inappropriate things.* She didn't say exactly what those things were but God saw her every action, heard her every word, knew her every thought. He knew how she loved the sense of adventure in challenging a new, forbidding land, just as He knew something about Burke drew her eyes to him more often than was appropriate.

Meggie yawned and stretched. She turned to see Jenny kneeling at her side and smiled as sweet as an angel. She patted Jenny's cheeks with her warm soft hands.

"Good morning, little miss. How are you this fine day?"

Meggie babbled excitedly.

"I'm sorry, sweetie. I don't understand."

Meggie caught Jenny's face between her palms and looked intently into her eyes and repeated the indiscernible words. Jenny couldn't look away from the intensity in the child's eyes. It filled her with sorrow that she was unable to understand what Meggie wanted.

Sounds came from the kitchen. Pots rattled. Boots scraped across the floor.

"I think we might have overslept. How about we get you dressed and then you can go see your uncle Burke."

Meggie had jumped from the bed at the idea of getting up but at the mention of her uncle, her face crumpled.

Jenny scooped her up before she started to cry. "Your uncle Burke would like to play with you. Wouldn't that be fun? Perhaps you could show him your dolly." As she talked, she slipped the nightgown over Meggie's head and pulled on her clean dress. Quickly she put on socks and tied the little boots. As soon as she released Meggie, the child grabbed her doll and hugged it close.

"Do you think you'd like to show her to Uncle Burke?"

Meggie shook her head.

"That's fine." It would take time but that was

first on her agenda. Right alongside urging Burke to hurry and resolve his differences with his fiancée. She ignored the way her heart quivered at the idea. She pushed resolve into her thoughts. Getting Meggie properly settled was her only concern.

Hand in hand, they stepped into the kitchen. Paquette stood at the stove, stirring a bubbling pot of porridge. Two huge frypans sizzled.

Burke put a bucket of foaming milk on the cupboard. Good. There would be milk for Meggie. That was essential.

"Good morning, Paquette, Burke." His name clung to her tongue. She forced herself not to duck away as he met her gaze, even though she knew her cheeks likely hinted at her awareness of him. She swallowed hard and dismissed those awkward, wayward feelings.

Intending to begin the way things should continue, she turned to Meggie, still clinging to her hand. "Meg, say hello to Paquette and your uncle Burke."

Meggie's chin quivered. Her eyes glistened but she read Jenny's silent insistence. They'd done battle before. Meggie knew she'd have to give in eventually so made the wise choice to do so from the beginning.

"'Lo, Pa—" She stumbled on the name, shot Jenny a look.

Jenny nodded encouragement.

Meggie tried again. "Pa—et."

Paquette chuckled.

Jenny waggled Meg's hand and indicated she should greet Burke.

Meg gripped Jenny's hand hard and hung her head. "'Lo Unca Burke."

Burke knelt to Meggie's level. "Hello to you, too, little Meggie. Did you sleep well?"

Meggie nodded without looking at her uncle. Burke shifted his gaze to Jenny. From this position she could see how his black hair glistened, how slight waves formed across the top of his head. Then she realized he'd spoken to her asking how she'd slept.

She cleared her throat and hoped he'd think her hesitation was from being thirsty or anything except the truth—she'd again been distracted by her wayward thoughts. "Well. Thank you."

He rose slowly, holding her gaze as he did. Her heart rose with him, pushing against her ribs as if wanting to rush out into open space. "Heard some crying," he murmured.

She nodded, forcing her gaze to leave his face and return to Meggie's upturned, watchful face. Meggie held her doll in one hand, watching them with an expectant look. "I think she wants you to say hello to her doll."

Burke blinked.

Jenny grinned. "It's a great honor." It somehow

pleased her to see this tough cowboy faced with the challenge of a little girl and her doll.

To his credit, Burke knelt again and touched the doll gently. "Is this your baby?"

Meggie nodded and allowed him to stroke the yarn hair on her precious dolly.

"She's very nice, isn't she?"

"My dolly." She cradled the toy against her neck and stuck her fingers in her mouth.

Jenny suspected Lena would have scolded her daughter for sucking her fingers but Jenny had decided to overlook it, allowing the child whatever comfort it provided.

Burke studied his niece a moment more. She considered him with equally serious intent. Neither of them made any motion toward the other.

His quiet caution around Meggie, giving her space to get used to her new surroundings, gave Jenny another moment's struggle with the reactions of her heart.

Burke straightened. Her eyes followed him, never leaving his face. Meggie pulled away and climbed up at the table to play with her doll.

"She's very attached to it, is she?"

Jenny struggled to make her tongue work, to bring her thoughts back to where they belonged. Seeing Burke with such interest was definitely not where they should be. What would Pa think if he could see her, read her thoughts?

Sudden guilt dried her mouth. She'd promised to marry Ted and yet here she stood with her heart pounding, her pulse racing at the sight of another man.

Hot regrets at her foolishness made it easy to turn her attention to Burke's question. "She's very fond of it. Lena made it for her just before she got ill. In fact, she put the finishing touches on it when she was almost too weak to work."

"That makes it extra special." His voice held a rough note as if his throat threatened to close off, which only made Jenny forget her resolve to keep her thoughts on practical things. A man who made room for emotions, who honored the effort that went into creating a pretty doll, touched a chord deep inside Jenny, making her want to laugh and cry at the same time.

Burke cleared his throat. "I better get back to the chores."

Jenny nodded and turned to Paquette. "What can I do to help?" She didn't look back until she heard the door close and Burke's boots thud on the veranda floor.

"You not work. You company." Paquette watched Jenny without looking directly at her. She'd refused help before. Suggested Jenny expected to be waited on. Jenny realized Paquette was somehow testing her.

"I'm not company. I'm only here on an errand. What kind of person would I be if I sat around instead of helping?" She rubbed her hands together. "Do you want me to fry the bacon?"

Paquette moved to one side, allowing Jenny to stand at the stove. The fat spattered. "Oh, I should have brought an apron."

Paquette reached under the cupboard and brought out a big apron made from white flour sacking but decorated with a red and gold geometric pattern. "Wear dis, you."

"Thank you." Jenny examined the design. "This is beautiful. Did you do it?"

"I learn from ma mere. She use beads and quills. I use…" She sought for a word. "From plants."

"Dyes?"

"Oui."

Jenny hesitated. "It's too nice to use for frying bacon."

Paquette laughed, a merry sound unlike the usual chortle. "It can wash."

So Jenny reluctantly donned the apron feeling she had stepped into another world, one full of adventure and excitement, bold cowboys and women with strange accents. She was dangerously close to stepping over a line she had firmly drawn for herself, one forbidding her to follow wayward paths, yet she couldn't keep back a smile as she turned the meat.

A few minutes later the men trooped in for breakfast. Jenny had the table set, the bacon fried, the bread sliced and piled high. She'd made coffee under Paquette's guidance while the other woman fried potatoes and eggs.

Jenny had thought of claiming a place at Paquette's side. After all, didn't she need to be available to help the woman? But she couldn't make herself do so. No matter where she sat, she would be aware of Burke with every beat of her heart and every breath she sucked into her tight lungs. Sitting next to him would enable her to encourage a friendship between him and Meggie and so she settled in the place she'd sat the night before.

Again the men reached for food as soon as everyone sat. Paquette cleared her throat. Everyone stopped, suddenly remembering Jenny's request for grace.

"Who's going to pray this morning?" Burke asked.

Dug shook his head. "I did it last night. It's someone else's turn."

The others mumbled.

Amused at how this was like a bunch of young boys arguing about whose turn it was, Jenny ducked her head to hide her smile.

Mac sighed loudly. "I'll say the words rather than starve to death."

Jenny snorted as she tried to contain her laughter.

Mac, beside her, grunted. "I know how to pray. Me old mam taught me." He bowed his head and murmured, "May God be with you and bless you. May you see your children's children. May you be poor in misfortune, rich in blessings. May you know nothing but happiness from this day forward. Amen." He sucked in air like he had forgotten to breathe throughout the recitation. "Pass the bacon, please."

Jenny stared. It was the most unusual grace she'd ever heard. "That was beautiful." God's blessing. Children's children. Happiness. No doubt what they all wanted.

She couldn't meet Burke's eyes even though she felt him watching her. She didn't want him to see the ache she knew would be evident. Didn't want to acknowledge it. God's blessing required obeying her parents. *Honor thy father and mother that thy days on the earth might be long.* Sometimes it was hard to quench her rebellious spirit. Remembering how often she'd failed to do so and the near disastrous consequences of one such time, she prayed for a submissive spirit.

The meal was almost over. She had to begin implementing her plans. Her heart had settled and she could face Burke without revealing anything but a calm, disciplined spirit. "Perhaps you would give us a tour of the ranch after breakfast." She rushed on before he could say anything. "I need to familiarize Meggie with her new home and teach her safe boundaries. As well, it would give you two a chance to get to know each other."

"Not a problem." He seemed unconcerned, as if this day was like any other. Hadn't he felt any of the emotions she had at Mac's prayer?

Of course, he hadn't. Why should she expect he would? He'd made no secret of what he wanted—her to be gone as soon as possible. Only she was foolish enough to want something more—something completely out of her reach.

She resolutely pushed aside a dying dream of adventure, excitement—why should she long so for things she couldn't have? It was this country. The open spaces grabbed her heart and wrenched out her childish dreams, pouring them into the sunshine like a stream of golden honey. When she returned home, she would realize how foolish all this was. "I'll help Paquette clean the kitchen first."

"Fine. Come outside when you're ready and I'll meet you."

It was all Burke could do to walk calmly from the house, the men at his heels. Everything in him

wanted to race away from the warmth of the kitchen
and the snarl of his thoughts. Mac's prayer had almost
been his undoing—God's blessing, children's children? Where was God's blessing in Burke's life? He
certainly hadn't seen any evidence of it. First, the
fiasco with Flora and now Lena dead.

His gaze had rested on Jenny. Something about
her made him remember his big dreams of a short
time ago—home, blessings, family.

He shifted his gaze to Meggie. This was his family.
He supposed that was a blessing from God. Yes, of
course it was. Only somehow it didn't satisfy.

"Where's the fire, boss?" Lucky asked.

Burke realized how fast his steps had become and
slowed. "No fire."

"Maybe anxious to get back to that little gal?"
Mac's teasing always sounded so serious that many
took offense.

Purposely misunderstanding, Burke said, "I'll
need to spend some time with Meggie getting to
know her so she'll be happy here." He pretended
he didn't notice the sly glances the men exchanged.
Every one of them knew Mac hadn't meant Meggie.
It didn't matter. They'd soon enough realize Jenny
and he would part ways. He ignored the ache twisting through his gut at the knowledge. "Dug, you ride
out and bring in the rest of the horses. We need to
get them broke before fall round up. Mac, check the

pasture to the north. Lucky, see if there's any hay to cut south of here."

He strode to the barn, leaving the men to follow his orders. In the dark interior he could think of nothing he came for. The cow was out grazing, the cats had finished their milk and sat washing themselves in patches of sunlight.

"Jenny's waiting for you," Lucky called, his voice carefully neutral but Burke heard the men chuckling before they dispersed. Let them get as much fun out of this as they could. Not that he could stop them if he tried.

He scrubbed his hands on the thighs of his jeans and adjusted his hat then strode toward the house. This was only about Meggie. He needed to keep reminding himself.

He paused at the bottom of the steps and carefully kept his gaze on his niece. "What would you like to see first? The cats or the horses?" The mounts in the nearby corrals were used to people and posed no danger.

"Kitties?" Meggie sounded cautiously eager.

"Scads of 'em. Come along." He straightened and finally allowed himself to face Jenny. Her eager expression almost undid all his harsh self-talk. Oh to see that eagerness every morning, to share it about the ranch. Whoa. Stop right there. This was about Meggie, not him.

He stepped aside and waited for Jenny to descend. Meggie skipped along at their side as they headed for the barn.

"Tell me about your ranch," Jenny said.

Her words caught him off guard, left him struggling to find an answer. "We raise cows and horses," he said tentatively, not knowing if she wanted any more information.

"Your animals range free?"

"To some extent. Most of the ranchers let the animals roam, but with more and more settlers things are changing." He had his own ideas of how things should be done. "Most ranchers let their animals graze during the winter, too, but I think it's too risky."

"Why?"

Her eyes brimmed with interest and he willingly told her how he considered the risks of having them unable to find enough to eat if they should get a lot of snow. "Cows can't dig through the snow like horses or buffalo. I prefer to contain them closer to home and have hay ready to take out if there's a need."

"That's very forward thinking of you. How do the other ranchers react?"

How did she guess there were mixed feelings about the way he did things? "Some think I'm overly cautious. Survival of the fittest, they say, produces the strongest cows."

"I suppose there's something to be said for that, but still, cows are not created to survive certain elements."

He realized they had stopped walking and stood talking intently. For his part, he was lost in the interest and knowledge she showed.

Meggie had paused to examine a bug crossing their path.

"Let's see if the kitties are still around."

They reached the barn. Most of the cats had disappeared but the old mama cat still lay in the sun, enjoying her rest from her newly weaned kittens. This old cat was the tamest of the bunch, having been around since Burke first arrived, and having learned humans meant warm milk and a gentle rub behind her ears.

"Go slow, little Meg," he warned.

Meggie, who'd been about to pounce on the unsuspecting cat, stopped.

Jenny caught Meggie's hand and knelt at her side. "Let her get used to us first. After all, we're brand new here."

Good advice for befriending both human and animal.

Jenny held her hand out to the cat and called softly.

Old mama meowed but didn't move.

"She's lazy. Or maybe wore out. Just raised a bunch of kittens."

"Kitties?" Meggie looked around expectantly.

Burke laughed. "Three of them went to neighbors. The other two are wild. You wouldn't want to hold them." He wished now that there were tiny kittens available but he knew of none.

Meggie turned back to the mama kitty. Squatting down she jiggled forward in a funny little frog walk.

Burke grinned.

Meggie reached the cat and touched it with one finger. The cat meowed and purred, obviously glad for the attention.

Meggie plunked to her bottom and the cat wrapped paws about her leg. The little one giggled. Soon the two were busy being friends.

Jenny stood back at Burke's side. "This is good for her. There's something about pets that eases sorrow."

"Maybe I should get myself a new dog." He wanted to groan at the way he sounded, as if he had so much sorrow to deal with.

"I thought it strange there was no dog. Don't all ranches have one?"

"Mine died a few months ago."

"I'm sorry. How'd it happen?"

"Don't know. Just found him dead one morning."

Suddenly he remembered things he'd ignored. Old Boy had gone missing after one of Flora's visits. They found him dead out past the barn a day later. He looked a little beat up. They'd suspected coyotes. But knowing what he did about Flora now, he wondered—

Nah. She would never hurt the dog. Had no reason to.

"We lost a dog when I was about twelve. He and I were best friends. I told him all my secrets. Never loved another quite so much." She gave a little laugh. "Guess I outgrew pet friends."

He wanted to ask what kind of friends she had now. Was there a special someone in her life? But her life was none of his business. They would soon say their good-byes and never see each other again. He would not acknowledge any discomfort at the idea.

Something caught the cat's attention and she raced off, leaving Meggie teary eyed.

He reached for her hand. "Let's go see the horses."

Meggie studied the outreached hand for several seconds then slipped hers into his. So small. So soft. Made him feel ten feet tall that she trusted him enough to do this.

Jenny, at his other side, touched his arm, sending jolts of warmth to his heart. He could get used to this—a child at one side, a woman at the other. He ground his teeth at such foolishness.

"This is a big step for her," Jenny whispered.

"I know." Surely the hoarseness of his voice was due to the fact Meggie had taken his hand, not because Jenny had touched him. But deep in the recesses of his mind he couldn't deny one meant as much as the other.

He led them from the barn to the pasture fence and whistled. The half dozen horses still at home lifted their heads and trotted toward him.

"Me touch," Meggie begged as the horses crowded around.

"I'll lift you." She made no protest as he did, and love for this little gal filled him. He wanted to hug her but didn't for fear of frightening her. He felt Jenny watching him and met her gaze. Her eyes filled with warmth and love—for Meggie, of course. But something real and alive passed between them, a mixture of pleasure and pain. He didn't try and sort out the source of each but the reasons came anyway. Pleasure at sharing love of this tiny child, pain at knowing he would only share it with Jenny for a short time.

Jenny jerked away first, a pink color blushing her cheeks. She reached out a hand and touched each of the horses, stroking their heads, scratching behind their ears, giving them equal attention as she murmured sweet nothings to them.

At least she wasn't afraid of them nor did she complain about how they smelled. He used to tell Flora they smelled like horses. What did she expect?

One of the horses tried to nibble Meggie's hair. Meg squealed and buried her face against Burke's chest. Love roared through him. He would do everything in his power to protect this child.

Meggie realized what she'd done and squirmed to be put down.

Burke released her. Afraid his emotions would be blaring from his eyes, he wouldn't look at Jenny to see if she'd noticed. Instead, he turned toward the alley. "Do you want to see the rest of the buildings?"

"I want to see everything." She sounded so eager that he stole a glance at her. Her eyes shone, a smile wreathed her face. Suddenly she sobered. "Meggie needs to become familiar with her surroundings." She stared toward the outbuildings

He nodded. It was all about Meggie. He needed no reminder. Yet her words left him feeling strangely hollow.

Chapter Five

Jenny wanted to stuff a rag into her mouth. She'd revealed far too much eagerness. Allowed herself too much interest in the ranch. In the man who owned the ranch.

With firm determination she forced her thoughts back to her purpose—settling Meggie. She needed to find out about the fiancée and encourage Burke to go ahead with his plans so Meggie would have a suitable home.

But they arrived at a long low building—the bunkhouse.

"I should show Meggie the inside."

Jenny wondered at the hesitation in Burke's voice. She was curious to see Burke's quarters—where the men lived, she corrected herself. "I'd like to see, too."

Burke hesitated. "I warn you, it's the home of a bunch of cowboys."

"What do you mean?" She pictured beds covered with brightly colored blankets, saddles at the end of each bed, bridles hung from hooks on the wall between them. Likely a stove in the middle of the room with a table nearby and chairs circling it.

A slow release grin started and made its way across his mouth and deep into her heart. The man had a smile to melt every one of her good intentions. "I guess I'll let you discover for yourself." He opened the door and waved her in.

"Come and see where Uncle Burke sleeps, Meggie." Holding the little girl's hand made Jenny feel less like she'd entered forbidden territory.

The first thing she noticed was the mess. No colorful blankets—only tangled bedcovers. No saddles. No neatly hung bridles. Instead a jumble of tools and ropes as if things had been tossed aside and forgotten.

The second thing to hit her senses was the smell. It was all she could do to keep from gasping. She tried to control her breathing but couldn't contain a cough.

Burke chuckled. "Some of the men are so familiar with the smell of animals they claim they can't sleep without it."

"I'm surprised they can sleep in here. Period."

Jenny could have bitten her tongue. When would she learn to keep her thoughts to herself?

Burke shrugged. "I guess you get used to it."

She spun on him, her vow of self-control forgotten. Again. "Do you enjoy these conditions?"

His eyes grew wary. "I tolerate them."

"Why do you sleep here when you have a perfectly good house?"

"You and Meg are in one bedroom."

"Oh come on. No one has slept in there for ages." There was another room across the hall. She hadn't opened the door, expecting the same disarray.

"It's only been a few months."

"Really. I'd have said at least two years." Her curiosity raged. "Why did you move out?"

They had moved away from the bunkhouse to the clear, fresh air of the nearby pasture and stopped to lean on a rail fence. Burke's gaze sought the distance but Jenny directed her attention to him. She was not just curious; she wanted to know why things were not as she expected. Something was wrong here, hidden under a current of secrecy and more. For Meggie's sake she needed to find out what it was.

Burke sighed and slowly brought his gaze back from afar. He stared at the grass at his feet. "I suppose Lena told you about Flora?" He glanced at her.

"Your fiancée?"

"She was."

Was? But before she could shape or voice the questions roaring through her like wildfire, he sucked in air.

"Flora stayed with a lady in town most of the time. Circumspect, she said. But she came for visits, staying a few days at a time. I gave her the third bedroom and moved out here." His voice was soft, as if he had gone back to his memories.

Jenny sensed that to say anything, ask any of her burning questions, would make Burke stop talking so she forced herself to remain quiet. But after a few minutes she decided he wasn't going to say more. "But you said no one has stayed there for months. What happened? What did you argue about?"

"Nothing." He drew his mouth down in a fierce frown. "Or maybe everything, though I didn't realize it at the time. She didn't want to marry until she got used to the place. Maybe I hurried her too much."

"I'm sure it's not too late to mend your fences, so to speak."

At the look in his face, she drew back. Anger. Frustration. Defeat. And then amusement. "Believe me. It's too late."

"You need to reconsider. For Meggie's sake. She needs a mother—"

He made a harsh sound. "Once Meggie gets used to me we'll do just fine. Be assured, Flora won't be coming back." His whole face tightened. "I have no need of a wife."

Jenny couldn't find a response. She would not admit that a tiny part of her—a corner of her heart not brought into submission—was glad he seemed so certain Flora no longer had any part in his life. She scolded herself. It made no difference to her. In a few days she would be back home and shortly thereafter announcing her engagement to Ted.

Shouldn't she have felt something besides resignation at the idea? It was only because this place was so far removed from her real life that the two couldn't coexist in her mind. Once she returned, she would realize this was only a dream. But what didn't change were Meggie's needs and her promise to Lena to see her daughter properly cared for. "Someone needs to take care of Meggie."

Slowly he faced her, such coldness in his eyes she almost stepped back. Only her stubborn nature enabled her to meet his gaze without flinching.

"I am perfectly capable of caring for her."

"But—"

"I'll hear no more argument on the matter." He turned and called Meggie. "I'll take you back to the house."

Anger roared through her. How did he think he could care for a two-year-old and run a ranch? She reached for Meggie's hand. "I can find my own way, thank you very much." She hurried away as fast as Meggie's little legs allowed.

Partway back she realized the humor of her situation. She'd asked God to keep her thoughts pure. To help her remember her promises. She'd thought it would be a fight to deny her attraction to Burke but his rude behavior had cured her. She laughed. God had uniquely answered her prayer. But by the time she reached the steps she didn't feel so much like laughing as crying. She only wanted to help. Keep her promise to Lena. Burke had no need to act like she'd done something wrong.

She went inside and begged Paquette for a job.

"Clean veranda, you?"

"I'd love to." She hurried out to tackle the job, leaving Meggie playing in the kitchen. She sorted out bits of harness and hung them from nails. She tossed the boots to the ground, carted shovelfuls of debris to the ash pile back of the house and set fire to it.

She had swept the floor and was on her hands and knees with a bucket of sudsy water and a brush when she heard the thunder of approaching animals and the whistles of men driving them. Leaving her task, she hurried around to watch. Burke threw open the corral gate and Dug drove a herd of horses into the pen. The horses milled around, tossing their heads, manes and tails catching the wind. Black horses, every color of red, a couple of buckskins and two or three pintos.

Jenny laughed softly as excitement coursed through her veins. It was glorious. So much power. So much activity.

Burke dragged the gate shut behind the last horse. Jenny couldn't make out his words as he called to Dug who edged toward the gate. Burke opened it enough to let him ride through then climbed up to sit on the top rail. Lucky joined them and the three men pointed and nodded.

Jenny wished she could hear what they said about the horses, wished she could join them and be close enough to feel the surge as the horses milled about.

After a few minutes, Dug moved away, taking his horse to the barn. Burke watched the wild bunch a bit longer. Jenny told herself it was the animals she couldn't take her eyes from but it was Burke she watched. Why was he so set against marriage? No. That wasn't what she meant. Why was he so set against making up with Flora? Her thoughts bounced around inside her head as if seeking an open door and escape. Regret warred with hope. Caution fought with adventure. Her thoughts were wayward children needing discipline. How often had both Ma and Pa warned her she must learn to control them? She sucked back air until her lungs released then returned to scrubbing the veranda floor. Several times she paused to listen to the horses whinny and neigh but she would not allow herself to return to the side of the house to watch the activity.

Only later, after the men had eaten dinner, full of talk about the horses, and after Meggie had fallen asleep for her afternoon nap, did Jenny slip around the veranda until she could see the pen.

The men seemed to be sorting out the animals. She wished she knew why they were put in different pens. Finally there was only one in the main pen.

Burke threw his lasso around the remaining horse and snubbed the end of the rope to a post before the rearing animal could jerk it from his hands. He edged toward the wild-eyed thing, speaking calmly.

Dug stood by with a blanket and saddle.

Burke intended to ride the horse!

Jenny's heart leapt to the back of her throat and stayed. She slipped from the veranda and, hoping no one would notice, crossed the yard until she pressed herself against a large post, hiding from view as best she could. She didn't want to draw attention to herself but she would not miss a moment of this drama.

Burke deftly drew the rope tighter until the horse couldn't rear. He snagged the blanket from Dug and eased it to the horse's back.

From where she stood, Jenny saw how the animal's eyes widened and its nostrils flared. It quivered all over.

Burke waited a moment, all the time talking softly. She couldn't make out his words but his tone of voice was soothing. A man in control. A man who knew how to still fears. A man—

Stop those wrongful thoughts.

Burke eased the saddle from Dug and gently lowered it to the horse's back. When he reached under the belly for the cinch, Jenny's lungs stopped working completely and refused to start again until the saddle was secured and Burke stood back safe and sound. Even then her breath jerked past tense muscles.

He managed to get on a bridle.

He caught the saddle horn.

Every muscle in Jenny's body quivered as he swung into the saddle.

"Let him go."

Dug released the rope and the horse exploded, head down, hind legs in the air.

She flinched with every pounding jump but Burke held the saddle like he was glued there. Her tension shifted from fear to excitement and admiration. She no longer watched the horse. Her eyes were on Burke. The alertness in his face as if anticipating every move, the set of his jaw, the way his arms exerted such control...

Her eyes burned with longing. Her throat tightened. Oh, if only she could be part of this every day.

The horse stopped bucking.

Dug yelled. "Way to show who's boss."

Jenny clapped and cheered. Then she clamped her palm against her mouth. She hadn't meant to reveal her presence. Did a lady hang about the corrals watching cowboys break horses? She didn't expect they did and could almost hear Ma's soft admonition. But it was too late to slip away. Burke had seen her and smiled.

She needed to explain herself. "It's the first time I've seen someone break a horse."

"These horses are already broke for the most part. Just haven't been rode in a while so they pretend they've forgotten." He patted his mount's neck. "Just trying to see if I'm still boss."

She knew her eyes shone with excitement, admiration and things she wouldn't confess even to herself. "Will you ride them all like this?"

"Me or one of the boys. It's not hard work."

She'd seen the pounding his body took. Looked like hard work to her. Hard and thrilling. "I wish—" She stopped before she could say how much she'd like to try riding a wild horse.

"If you ever want to ride, let one of us know and we'll saddle up a quiet horse."

"I might like that."

Dug cleared his throat. "Hey, boss, did you forget there's more horses? You want me to ride 'em?"

Burke blinked as if caught at something he shouldn't have been doing.

Jenny had the same guilty feeling. "I better check on Meggie." She picked up her skirt and hurried to the house.

Burke watched her go. She'd observed the whole time. He'd seen her slip across and hide behind the post as if she didn't want anyone to notice her. He noticed all right. With every thought and every nerve ending. She was like a magnet drawing from him feelings he didn't know he owned. Didn't want to deal with. It had taken every ounce of his self-control to keep his attention on riding the horse.

And then she'd clapped and cheered. He knew by the way she covered her mouth she hadn't intended to and it thrilled him more than riding the horse to know he'd managed to edge past her cool exterior. What else lay beneath? What was she really like?

Stupid thoughts. He needed to rope them and ride them into submission.

Instead he watched until she disappeared inside the house.

"She's different, boss," Dug said.

"Different than what? Old cheese? Fresh bread?" He hoped his tone would tell Dug to cease.

Dug only laughed. "Different than that other one."

Seems the men couldn't bring themselves to say Flora's name. Not that he could blame them. Flora had been rude and nasty to them. And that was at her best.

"Flora was different, too, to start with."

Dug was silent—not an easy silence.

Burke turned to see the stubborn look on his face. "What?"

"You only tried to tell yourself it was so."

"I tried to tell myself lots of things." That she would change. That he could persuade her she'd get used to things. He no longer believed it and wouldn't try and convince himself or someone else ever again. "Let's get another horse."

He needed to work away his foolishness and he rode horse after horse until his whole body ached. Still every time he paused, his thoughts headed for the house to wonder what Jenny was doing.

He should pack his saddlebags and head out into the distance. He could check the herd. Explore the countryside—

But he couldn't. He now had a little girl to look after. Things would be a great deal more complicated when Jenny left and Meggie became his sole responsibility. Of course, Paquette would help as much as she could.

He needed to stop worrying. Meggie would adjust quickly and as she grew older, she would learn how to look after herself. Why, by the time she was three, she'd be riding all over with him. Maybe he'd see if he could find a small pony for her....

Jenny wished she could avoid Burke. It seemed the only way she might hope to control her thoughts. But even when she couldn't see or hear him, her thoughts wouldn't be so easily controlled.

And then there was Meggie. The sooner she got Meggie used to things, the sooner she could leave. She had hoped to see a more suitable arrangement concerning Meggie's care, but Burke was her guardian and it was up to him to see to that. She ignored the pricks of her conscience that said Lena expected more.

She could only do so much. She shivered as she admitted her weakness—how this adventure pulled at her thoughts, how Burke was a magnet to them.

She needed to return home before she did anything foolish she'd regret the rest of her life.

Over the next few days, they settled into an uneasy routine. After the evening meal Burke and Jenny would take Meggie for a walk. First, they visited the cats. If it was cool enough they strolled down the trail away from the house; otherwise they wandered about the yard, pausing to speak to the horses or the men.

Jenny often waited until Meggie was asleep for

another walk, which took her down the path to the open prairie. She loved the open plains, especially in the evening. Sometimes Burke joined her. Like tonight.

To keep her thoughts from running in forbidden directions she spoke of her family. "Mary is a year older. She got married last fall." She'd married John Stokes, a man Ma and Pa fully approved of. So many evenings she had overheard their conversation—John is steady. He'll be good for Mary. A man with a solid future. She heard the unspoken words—they feared their daughters would choose unwisely and suffer a dreadful future. She understood their concern. But sometimes a safe and solid life threatened to imprison her. Surely it was only her current situation—so foreign and exciting—that made it so difficult to control her thoughts. She pulled them firmly back to obedience and continued telling of her sisters.

"Sarah is fifteen." She chuckled. "Going on eighteen. I think she's been trying all her life to catch up to Mary and me." They were a strange trio of sisters. Mary wanting only to be like Ma and Pa. Jenny longing for adventure and excitement and little Sarah trying to grow up too fast.

"Tell me how you met Lena."

"The first Sunday they came to church I introduced myself. We just seemed to suit each other. She was so full of life. Not afraid of anything." Only

Mark's opinion carried any weight with Lena. And then Meggie's needs became foremost. "She was a devoted mother right to her death." Jenny's voice thickened. She owed it to her best friend to follow her wishes to a tee. Who would care for Meggie when Jenny left? Paquette? She was fond of the child but so crippled she couldn't even lift her.

"Have you known Paquette a long time?" Perhaps he would replace her with someone who could manage the child.

"Since I arrived here."

"She come with the place?" Jenny wanted to know more about the woman and what options might be available.

Burke laughed.

It was the first time she'd heard him so amused and the sound roared through Jenny's defenses, leaving her struggling to keep from staring at him. Finally, in order to stifle the thrill bubbling to the surface, she bent, plucked a blade of grass and examined it with devout concentration. "Didn't realize I said anything amusing."

"This place didn't exist when I came out here. I've built it up from scratch." His voice rang with pride. "Nothing will make me leave here."

She wondered at the harshness in his voice. "Can't see why anyone would want you to." Her gaze swept the circle of the horizon.

"What do you see?"

A smile started in her eyes, spread to her mouth and smoothed her heart. "I see space. Opportunity." She allowed herself to meet his gaze. Knew immediately she'd made a mistake as his dark eyes sought and found entry into her heart. They regarded each other silently, exploring—

It was only because she envied him living out here in the open, inviting prairie. Nothing more. Nothing that knocked at forbidden doors in her mind.

She sought to escape her treacherous thoughts. When she felt in control, she straightened. "Paquette?" Did her voice sound as hoarse as it felt? "Where did you find her?" She tried to force herself to look some place other than into his eyes but she couldn't pull away. She realized what she'd said. Find. As if he'd gone looking for Paquette. Hopefully he would understand what she meant to say. "I mean where did she come from?"

His eyes creased with amusement. "You're right. I did find her. Literally. In a little shelter made of animal hides. She was so sick she couldn't walk and was on the verge of starving to death."

"How awful." The horror of the idea allowed her to shift her gaze away from his intense look. "Why was she alone?"

"She'd been abandoned by her Métis husband when she got sick."

"That's terrible. How could he walk away from her, leave her to die?"

Burke sighed. "I expect he figured she was going to die anyway so the best thing he could do was take care of himself."

Slowly, knowing she risked being caught in a struggle with her wayward thoughts, she brought her gaze back to him. "Is that how people out here feel?" She thought she knew the answer but wanted to hear it from his lips.

"A person ought to be prepared to deal with challenges, inconveniences, whatever they must, in order to fulfill their promises."

She nodded. "What sort of promises?"

"Like the promise of marriage, whether an engagement or a signed, sealed marriage."

His voice rang, conveying just how important this was. He would be shocked to know she'd once or twice over the past few days considered reneging on her promise to Ted—or more accurately to Ma and Pa.

Burke continued. "I think there are unspoken promises about family, too. Like Meggie. I will provide her a home no matter what it takes. And even this ranch. I've committed myself to it. What sort of man would I be if I simply walked away when things got tough?"

She couldn't speak as her mind whirled with

words—commitment, marriage, family—he was a man who faced challenges. Oh to stand at the side of such a man. Face those challenges together. Conquer them.

Firmly, with every ounce of discipline she'd been taught and tried so hard to learn, she pushed the ideas from her head. "So you rescued Paquette and gave her a home?"

"As soon as she got her strength back she took over running the house. She rules the roost."

"Is that what happened to Flora? Paquette wasn't willing to relinquish her position?" Somehow she couldn't see Burke allowing such a thing especially after what he'd just said about promise and commitment. But something had happened and the very fact he wouldn't speak of it made her unduly curious.

Burke snorted—a sound ripe with something she couldn't identify—perhaps bitterness or maybe mockery. "Flora had no objection to Paquette doing the work."

She stared at him, knowing her surprise showed in her eyes. "Was she overwhelmed by the work, then?"

"That's a good way to describe it. Yes, I guess you could say Flora was overwhelmed."

She waited, suspecting he meant something more than Flora was overwhelmed by work, but he seemed disinclined to explain. She ached to know. To understand the tension drawing his shoulders upward. Oh, if only she had the right to reach out and brush her hand across his arm and offer comfort.

But she did not. It would be well to remember that fact.

Chapter Six

Burke shifted so Jenny couldn't see his face as a blast of emotions swept through him. Disappointment that his plans had been thwarted. Sorrow at his loss, though he had to confess the loss of Lena far outweighed Flora's loss. Then determination settled over it all. As he said, he was committed to this ranch.

He'd let himself swim in the silent messages blaring from her brown eyes. Allowed himself to think what it would be like to share his love of the land, his determination to conquer it with a woman of like mind.

Hadn't he thought that's what he and Flora would be doing? They'd corresponded three years. She'd written words glowing with hope for a new life, a fresh start—as if life back East was not to her liking. Then she came for a visit. They'd planned for the visit to end in their marriage.

Overwhelmed? Guess that explained why she refused to help Paquette, refused to eat with the men. Why she shuddered when she looked at the prairie and why eventually she had run screeching across the land. Her screeching hadn't stopped even when he brought her back. The marshal said he'd seen it before. "Prairie madness," he'd called it and told stories of both men and women suffering the effects of days of loneliness and emptiness. Burke didn't see how loneliness applied to Flora. She had him, Paquette and the men. In the end it had been the land she couldn't take. He'd had no choice but to let the marshal take her to the insane asylum. She'd lasted two months out here.

Burke had never told Lena. Couldn't find the words to explain what happened.

Jenny touched his elbow. "I don't know what happened but I'm sorry it didn't work out."

Slowly he turned to face her, allowing himself to drink from the kindness in her eyes. Something shifted in his heart. He felt an uncertain hope for the first time in months.

Hope? He pretended it wasn't so. He didn't hope for anything but success in running the ranch. And now being Meggie's guardian. Nothing more. Not God's help nor any woman's help. "I demanded too much from her. I won't make that mistake again."

Something closed behind her eyes as if she didn't

want him to guess at her thoughts. "Not everyone would be overwhelmed by this country."

Again hope swept through him. If only—he shook his head, driving such thoughts into nothingness.

"What about Paquette?" she persisted, as if she must prove a point. "She's survived this country even when she was ill and abandoned."

"She's born and bred in the wilds and even then, it almost destroyed her."

"Then what will happen to Meggie?"

"She'll be raised to survive."

Jenny turned away to stare out at the darkening landscape. "Seems to me you're expecting failure from all women just because Flora somehow failed."

"Not all women. Just eastern-raised ones. This is not a life for them."

She spun to face him, her eyes blazing. "I don't think you are equipped to make that kind of decision for others. After all—" She clamped her mouth shut. Then she headed toward the house, her breath rushing in and out so hard he feared she would pass out.

He strode after her. "No reason for you to take this personal, is there?" Did she love the prairie and wish she could help tame it? Hope again reared its persistent head.

She slowed considerably. "Of course not but it's still presumptuous on your part."

"Maybe." But she hadn't said anything to indicate how she felt or to give him any basis for his flagging hope. Even though he could easily catch up to her and walk at her side, he stayed several feet behind, as he reasoned his way back to the truth—words were easy. Even Flora had no trouble writing the right thing. But living the life was far different. Overwhelming, as Jenny said. "I'll say good night here. I have things to tend to." He didn't wait for her to answer but headed for the corrals as if he could outrun his thoughts.

"Good night," she called.

Next morning, he watched her more closely than usual. She helped Paquette. Did she do it out of a sense of obligation or did she enjoy the work as much as she seemed to?

She normally took Meggie for a walk after breakfast and he hung about outside until she showed up then joined her. He didn't miss the way Dug chortled as if this simple event meant impending wedding bells.

He told himself it was only so he could spend time with Meggie. But he knew it was far more. Something about Jenny had drawn him from the beginning and now her comments about some women not being overwhelmed had him curious. Did she mean herself?

And if she did?

Only curiosity made him want to know. It wouldn't

make any difference to his decision. Would it? He couldn't answer the question. Instead he fell in at her side. "She's settling in well, isn't she?" He nodded toward Meggie.

"Yes, I think she is."

Meggie caught his hand and pulled him toward the barn. She pointed to the opening for the loft. "Kitties."

He understood immediately what she wanted. All the cats had disappeared. She'd noticed they often went that direction. He made a low whistling.

Meggie laughed. "More."

He did it again.

Meggie held out her arms. He lifted her. When she allowed him to hug her, his love for her burned through him, stinging his eyes.

"'Gain," she said, touching his lips.

He chuckled, which of course made it impossible to whistle. At her insistence, he sobered and again made the sound.

Mama cat meowed as she came to the familiar call.

"Kitty." Meggie almost launched herself from his arms.

"Hold on there, little miss." He released her so she could go to the cat.

"She's certainly warming up to you."

"That's good." He avoided looking at Jenny,

feeling slightly foolish at how tight his lungs were and how his eyes stung at Meggie's acceptance.

Meggie had a routine she insisted they follow so they moved on a few minutes later to greet the horses, then she raced down the trail until she found something on the ground to study.

"She's settling so well, I'll soon be able to leave."

Leave? The idea seared his mind. "No need to rush away." They walked side by side in Meggie's wake. He didn't dare look at her for fear he would reveal how much he wanted her to stay.

"My family might not agree."

"Only your family?" The question hung between them.

"Pa has picked out someone for me. I promised to give my answer when I return."

He stumbled a bit. Not enough for Jenny to notice and wonder what had tripped him when the ground was worn and smooth beneath his feet. Picked out? Promised? "Does that mean you haven't made up your mind?"

She didn't speak for so long he turned to study her and watched determination replace confusion. "Pa knows what's best for me." For one fleeting second she met his eyes. He would have said she seemed regretful. And then she jerked her chin upward. "I'll accept his choice. I'll say yes."

"You're letting your father pick out your husband?" Doing so wasn't unusual. But it didn't seem to fit what he'd learned about Jenny. "I thought you were more self-sufficient. More…" He sought for a word to describe the way she swung her arms over her head, the way she clapped when he broke a horse, the way she asked questions about the ranch, the way she touched dark corners of his heart, made him hope for things he thought were over. "I guess I took you for a woman with lots of grit." He knew his sentence ended on a bitter note. He had only himself to blame that he'd let thoughts of the future include her. She'd certainly never given him any reason for hope.

"It is sometimes a mistake to follow your own wayward heart. Doesn't God warn us that 'our hearts are deceitful above all things, and desperately wicked'?" Satisfied with her explanation, she nodded. "I prefer to trust God for the details of my life. I believe He is concerned about them and sends guidance through my parents and…other means, too, of course."

He wanted to argue but he couldn't. God seemed little interested in guiding the details of his life and yet following his heart had proven to be a mistake. Still—

"I guess if you love him." Speaking the words felt like arrows striking his soul.

"Ted's a good man."

Ted. The man had a name. He wished he didn't

know it because he disliked him for absolutely no reason. Other than he was a good man. Good enough for Jenny to choose to marry. "I better get to work." He strode away so fast his boots kicked up clouds of dirt.

The truth could not be avoided. Jenny was anxious to get back home. She only needed to be reasonably certain Meggie would be fine without her. He lifted his face to the sky. Did God delight in manipulating the affairs of man to see their reaction? To see them bleed with sorrow? Wilt with unfilled hopes? He would never understand why God allowed bad things to happen.

Such questions were too profound for him. He had to accept that God ruled the universe but seemed to have little concern for the everyday little things of puny man. Not that he blamed God. He must get tired of the way people messed up.

Well, Burke didn't plan to mess up again. An eastern-born woman did not belong out here where there was nothing to see except the horizon on all sides and where life required day after day of unrelenting labor.

The sooner Jenny left, the better for them all.

He needed a plan for getting Meggie settled into ranch life so Jenny could go home to her Ted.

* * *

Meggie lay stretched out, snoring gently. Her afternoon nap usually lasted an hour or two.

Restless, Jenny wandered outside. No men lingered about. That was just fine. She didn't want to see Burke. Things had shifted between them since she'd told him about Ted. Though in reality she'd said very little about him. But Burke insinuated she was somehow weak in following Pa's advice. But why should she care if Burke seemed disappointed with her? She knew her own weaknesses, knew God, in His almighty, infallible wisdom, had given her a father to guide her.

She wandered toward the corrals. Many of the pens were empty. The men had taken some of the horses they'd broken and moved them to another pasture. But behind the barn she found one horse alone. A big horse black as polished coal. "You're a pretty one, aren't you?"

The horse reared and snorted, backing into the far corner.

"Got to put on a good show, do you? I know how you feel. Lots of times I feel like I have to put on a good show, too."

The horse tossed his head.

"I guess I don't know what kind of show I'm putting on right now. Am I pretending to be an obedient daughter, an obedient Christian when I long for adventure?" She thought of sharing life with a man like Burke. Her heart kicked into a gallop. Despite her resolve, she was drawn toward him, aching for the chance to work side by side in conquering this land, establishing a successful ranch. "You know what?" She waited for the animal to paw the ground as if asking for an answer. "I think I'm just confused because I'm so far away from home and everything here is new and exciting."

The horse waggled his head as if agreeing.

"You, too?"

Jenny chuckled to herself.

"I should write a letter home telling them I've arrived safely and explaining I'll have to delay my return until I'm satisfied Meggie will be provided for as Lena and Mark would want."

Soft noises from the horse made her laugh.

"You're a regular font of wisdom. Come here and let me pat you." But the big black animal shook his head as if saying no. "Fine. Maybe next time. Now I'm off to write a few words." She hesitated. "Nice talking to you." Laughing, she returned to the house and penned a letter. She didn't know when she'd get a chance to mail it but she felt better after she'd written to Ma and Pa.

When Burke came in to fill his canteen she asked when she could hope to post the letter. "Dug will go to town Saturday night. He'll be glad to take it. He picks up any mail for the ranch at the same time." His words were clipped as if he had too much work to deal with her questions.

Fine. She wasn't here to be amused.

She spent the rest of the afternoon pulling weeds from around the house.

She would have skipped the evening walk but Meggie insisted. Her disappointment that Burke didn't join them far outreached reasonable. "He needs to spend more time with Meggie," she murmured to the silent prairie.

Next morning as soon as breakfast was finished, Burke turned to his niece. "Meg, do you want to go with me today?"

Jenny wondered if he had read her thoughts of the previous evening and decided to act on them.

"Me go." Meg jumped down and headed for the door.

"Hang on. I'm not quite ready." He turned to Jenny, his expression hooded so she couldn't guess at his thoughts. "It's time Meggie and I got used to spending our day together."

She nodded, hoping she hid her feelings as well as he. "Where are you taking her?"

"I thought I'd show her more of the ranch. After all, it's to be her home."

Jenny stomped back an unreasonable burst of

jealousy. No one had offered to show her more of the ranch. Of course they hadn't. She was here to get Meggie settled. Nothing more. "How far will you walk?" Maybe he'd ask her to accompany them.

"We'll ride."

Ride? "But she's only two."

"How old do you think children are when their parents pack them across the country to start a homestead?"

What that had to do with taking Meggie for the day, Jenny couldn't begin to comprehend. She studied her empty dish. Remembered a lady did not vent all her feelings. Recalled Ma's word to temper her reactions.

Apparently Burke took her silence for acquiescence. "Would you like that, little Meg? To ride with your uncle?"

"I ride." She pulled at his hand, urging him to come.

"It's settled then." He paused at Jenny's side. "We'll be back for dinner."

"Dinner?" she murmured. That was five hours away.

"Sooner or later we have to learn to get along without you. Best get at it." He strode away, his words like bees stinging at her thoughts. Plainly, he couldn't wait for her to leave.

"Man not know babies," Paquette mumbled.

Her words did nothing to soothe Jenny's concerns. But she was powerless to stop Burke from taking Meggie anywhere he chose. As she helped Paquette clean the kitchen, she watched Burke ride from the yard, Meggie perched in front of him babbling away excitedly.

Burke noticed her at the window and nodded curtly.

She ducked her head and gave undue attention to the pot she scrubbed. Of course she had to leave. The sooner the better. But for him to be so eager for it....

Well, what did she expect? From the first day, even before he'd known who she was, he'd said this was no place for a woman. Seems he still believed it.

Not that it mattered. She had other plans.

But the ache filling her almost drove her to her knees. She rushed to her room and flung herself on the bed to gasp for air. Finally calm, she prayed for God's strength to guide and uphold her. *And keep Meggie safe. Help her adjust to her new life.*

On the other hand, if this went as poorly as Jenny feared it would, perhaps it was God's way of showing Burke he couldn't manage without a wife. Maybe if things didn't go well, he would consider being reconciled to Flora.

She fell back on the bed and again struggled for composure.

* * *

Meggie squirmed in Burke's arms, wanting to pet his mount. He held her so she could do so and she laughed.

"This is going to work out just fine, isn't it, Meg peg?" The two of them riding the range together, enjoying the land. She'd grow up to be a real little cowgirl.

They flushed out a pair of partridges.

Meggie squealed. "Birdies."

"Partridges. Good to eat." He pointed out other birds. An antelope watched them then raced away.

Meggie laughed and jabbed her finger in the general direction, almost falling from his arms in her excitement.

"Careful, little one." He chuckled. This was going to be a great morning. "Let's go find some cows."

"Cows?" She looked around. "No cows."

"Soon." Well-being slowly eased away the knot in his thoughts he'd been dragging around like something caught on his spur. But there remained twin ropes of regret and hopelessness that tightened every time he thought how Jenny would soon be able to go home to her Ted.

He would not let disappointment turn the day sour and urged his horse to a faster gait.

Meggie giggled as she bounced.

"You're a natural little cowgirl."

They rode up an incline and he stopped to look around, trying to pinpoint clusters of cows.

"Down please."

"Not yet. See those cows way over there? We'll stop when we get to them."

Meggie stiffened. "Down."

"Not yet, Meggie." She wasn't used to riding. He'd let her take a break when they reached the little grove of trees where some cows grazed.

Meggie settled back for the ride. A good kid. She'd adapt quickly. Before they reached their destination, she started to whine. "Want down. Want down."

"Soon."

His promise did not make her patient. By the time they reached the trees, her fussing had sent the cows racing away. Burke struggled to hold her. He swung from the saddle, scarcely able to keep her from squirming out of his grasp until he reached the ground.

She staggered a few feet as if her legs had forgotten how to work and then ran in wide circles waving and yelling. Something about her excitement reminded him of Jenny. She'd lifted her arms to the skies the first day she arrived at the ranch. Was it excitement she felt? She'd said it was presumptuous on his part to think all women would fail on the prairies. He'd thought long and hard on that. What did she mean? But there was no point in trying to decide if she thought she could be different. She'd be leaving as soon as possible and return to her Ted, handpicked for her by her pa. She wasn't any different than Flora. Flora retreated to a madhouse. Jenny would retreat to her father's plan and protection.

"Come on, Meg. It's time to move." He wanted to check the watering holes and run his eyes over the cattle and make sure they were all well.

Meggie dropped to the ground and wailed. "I want Mama."

Burke stared at the sobbing child. How did one deal with her cries for a mama she would never again see? Where did one get wisdom for such a situation? He could almost hear Jenny's voice telling him God was concerned with the details. He didn't buy it because if it were true, where was Lena? And why was Flora where she was?

He scooped the child into his arms and ignored her protests as he swung into the saddle.

After a moment she settled, glancing about with interest. He let out air that had grown stale in his lungs. This was all strange to her but she'd adjust.

A few miles later though, she started to squirm. "Go home. Wanna go home."

"Not yet. Soon."

She wailed. She threw her head back. Her cries intensified. He remembered her behavior on the train and his admiration for Jenny grew. How had she coped hour after hour? He didn't know if he could manage until noon. A glance toward the sun informed him he had at least two hours to go.

Never had a morning promised to be so long.

His leg suddenly felt warm. He lifted Meggie and saw a dark spot growing on his jeans. She'd wet herself. And him, too. "Meggie, why didn't you say something?"

She hung her head and sobbed.

"Never mind. We'll both just have to endure it until we get home."

An hour later, he admitted defeat and turned the horse toward the ranch. He thought he'd never get back. A hundred yards from the house Meggie's cries brought Jenny to the veranda, Paquette peering over her shoulder mumbling about the poor baby. At least Jenny held her tongue though her eyes spoke accusation. Lucky came to the barn door and shook his head as if to say Burke was a cruel guardian.

"She needs clean clothes." He handed the squalling child to Jenny. The smell had grown pungent. He reined around and headed for the bunkhouse. He needed a bath and clean clothes, too.

Lucky backed out of sight as Burke rode toward the corrals. "Look after my horse," Burke called, knowing the man could hear him even if he pointedly avoided him.

An hour later, he tramped back to the house

feeling restored by a soak in the metal tub behind the bunkhouse and a set of clean clothes. He took his place at the table. Mac was away tending to work but Dug and Lucky sat at the table, their gazes carefully averted. Jenny wasn't so cautious. The look she sent him practically left a brand. He sighed. "Who is going to say grace?" They'd all taken turns except him.

No one volunteered.

"Guess it's about your turn, boss," Lucky said, when it became apparent no one else was offering.

"Me?" The men gave him an unyielding stare. Jenny's gaze challenged him. Even Paquette silently warned him to expect no sympathy from her. He knew what was going on. They were all angry with him for making Meggie miserable. "Very well." He bowed his head. He didn't feel a lot of gratitude. Truth was, he didn't know exactly what he felt. God had been relegated to the ruler of the universe. Not concerned with the details of life. Yet didn't saying grace imply acknowledgement of His hand in the most basic of needs—food?

Lucky cleared his throat, reminding Burke they all waited.

Burke searched for something appropriate to say, remembered a verse his mother had taught him. "Heavenly Father, kind and good, thanks we offer for this food—" There was more—*for thy love and tender care, for all the blessings that we share*—but he couldn't give voice to the words. He had once believed them. No more. Was it because of Flora? Suddenly he realized he'd stopped thinking life was so simple after his parents died. That's when he began to doubt God's tender care. The events since had only served to entrench his belief more firmly. "Amen."

"Food be cold," Paquette complained but everyone else dug in without comment.

Burke, for his part, was content to eat without enduring any conversation. It had been a difficult morning. As if to emphasize the failure of his experiment, Meggie wouldn't meet his eyes or respond to anything he said.

It didn't require anyone to point out Meggie wasn't ready for accompanying her uncle on long rides. But he knew from the unblinking looks Jenny gave him she wouldn't be letting the episode go without saying something.

Somehow he suspected he wouldn't care for her observations. He sighed. Seemed the afternoon would be as unpleasant as his morning.

Chapter Seven

Meggie should have fallen asleep instantly but she fussed like she had the first day, as if reminded of all she'd lost. Jenny rubbed her back and sang to her. When she finally gave in to sleep, Jenny was exhausted but she had a task to tend to. She'd prayed God would use this to show Burke how much he needed a wife. Now she had to make sure Burke understood that's what it meant.

A glance out the kitchen window revealed no one about. No doubt Burke guessed she would tackle him on his outing with Meggie and had ridden off for the day. Well, he might delay it but he wouldn't avoid it. Sooner or later they must talk.

In the meantime she needed some company. She grabbed a carrot from the bin and headed to the corrals and her new friend. She'd named the big black horse Ebony. As she approached the pen, Ebony whinnied.

"Hello, big boy. Glad to see me, are you?" He seemed eager for her visits but still shied away from touching. Today she hoped to overcome his fear. She held out the carrot. "Look what I have for you. Come on." The horse quivered as he took a step closer. "That's a boy." Slowly, as she murmured, he crossed the pen, stopped almost within reach then raced away. "Come on. You know you want it." She shook the carrot. Again he started toward her. She talked softly. "Sometimes a person just has to confront their fears to discover they're all a mirage." That's what she hoped Burke would discover. Surely if he gave Flora another chance they could work things out. Ebony's lips brushed her fingers. Laughter bubbled up but she closed her mouth and held it in for fear of frightening the horse away. He took the carrot. She touched his muzzle. He quivered but didn't run. "Oh, you are a pretty thing, aren't you?" She ran her hand up his warm neck and scratched along his jaw.

"What do you think you're doing?" Burke roared.

She hadn't heard him approach and his angry voice made her yelp and jump. Ebony reared away snorting and tossing his head.

"Can't you see he's a renegade? He'd as soon stomp you as let you pass. Why, if this isn't just like a woman. Can't leave 'em a minute without them getting themselves into trouble."

Her alarm gave way to anger at being scolded as if she had done something so foolish it defied explanation. "We were doing just fine until you came along yelling your fool head off."

He grabbed her elbow and dragged her away from the pen. "Are you out of your head? He's a killer."

"Phew. He's a pet. Watch." She yanked from his grasp and headed for the pen. "Come on, Ebony. I won't let him hurt you. Come on, pretty boy."

She made two steps before Burke practically jerked her off her feet.

"Don't you ever listen to advice?" He scowled so hard his eyebrows almost touched.

She wondered if her own brows did the same. "I listen when the person giving it knows what he's talking about." She planted her fists on her hips and leaned forward. "You obviously do not."

He refused to give an inch. "Right. I've been ranching for four years and you? How long now?"

"Fine. If we're going to talk about experience let me ask you, how long have you been caring for two-year-olds? How many do you know who ride all day?"

He snorted but did not yield.

Her conscience pushed at her anger. This was no

way to convince him of what he needed to do. But right now she wanted only to—

To be part of his life.

Her anger fled—all fight defeated. She was never going to be that. "You're right. I sometimes forget to listen to advice." She'd paid for it in the past. Vowed she wouldn't pay for it in the future. "Pa is often telling me to listen to those older and wiser."

"I guess that explains why you're letting him choose your husband. Afraid to follow your heart. However—" He leaned closer so she felt each word on her cheeks. "That's not the same thing at all."

She fought her rebellious spirit and won. "But sometimes it is."

"Care to explain what's behind that statement?"

"I do not."

He snorted, sounding an awful lot like Ebony. Both afraid of too many things, both hiding it behind a tough exterior. "Should have guessed you'd be too self-controlled. A real lady. All eastern ways."

Fire burned through her veins at his mocking. It stung her eyes. "You know nothing about me."

"So tell me. What makes you so set on doing exactly what your father decides is best for you?" His voice softened. "Jenny, what do *you* want?"

His quiet question almost loosened her tongue. But what did he care what she wanted? Besides, what did she want except to see Meggie settled happily? Her anger died as suddenly as it flared. "Do you have time for a little walk?"

"Sure." He answered too quickly. Did he think she would answer his questions?

They turned down the path and headed away from the buildings. Jenny didn't speak, not certain how to broach the subject. *Father God, give me the right words. Help me say only what helps.*

They paused as they reached the end of the corrals. Jenny looked around, letting the wide-open spaces lift her heart and carry it along, soaring above the fragrant grass, almost touching the clouds. "I could never get tired of this view." She hadn't meant to speak the words aloud and rushed on before Burke noticed. "You said I should listen to advice. Are you willing to do the same?" She turned so she could watch his reaction. Caught a flash of something warm and promising before he understood her question and his expression turned cautious.

"I listen if it's wise."

"I don't claim to be wise but may I offer some advice anyway?" She didn't wait for his nod but appreciated it when it came. Willingness on his part made what she had to say easier. "I think you can see Meggie isn't ready to be a cowboy." Again a reluctant nod. "She needs a mother. Can I be so bold as to suggest you contact Flora and ask her to reconsider?"

No mistaking the dark thunder in his expression. "I'm afraid that's totally impossible."

"Nothing can be that bad. Whatever your disagreement, if you talk I'm sure you can resolve things."

He sucked in air until she feared he'd sweep up the dust from the trail. Then he let it out in a gust that would surely move leaves if there had been any on the path. "In this case I am sorry to say you are wrong. It is that bad."

She shook her head preparing to argue.

He grabbed her elbow and shook her gently. "Flora is in an asylum." His eyes were cold though she detected pain behind the anger.

"Asylum?" Sick or—

"She's insane."

Jenny gasped. "No."

"I was returning from my last visit to her that day on the train."

She thought how she'd been attracted to him even then, knowing it was wrong of her. And though it was still wrong, her heart reached for him in a way that both frightened and thrilled her.

"Her parents were there. They told me not to come again. My visits visibly upset Flora. They said a lot more."

At the pain in his voice, she squeezed his elbow, felt his tension. Oh if only she could somehow ease his sorrow.

"They blamed me but no more than I blame myself. From the beginning she was afraid of the prairie. Said it was too lonely. Too empty. Said it sucked at her insides. I wouldn't listen. I figured she'd get used to it. Instead—" He shook his head. "It was awful. The way she screamed and wailed. It took two men to get her into a buggy. The last sound I heard was a shriek. I will never forget it."

"That explains why you think this country is no place for a woman."

"It isn't."

"Oh, Burke. Not everyone sees lonely and empty when they look out there." Without breaking eye contact she tilted her head toward the prairie. "Some find it exciting." She stopped. Explaining her reaction to the land would serve no purpose. "Don't blame yourself. Don't condemn others."

His gaze drove deep into her soul as if seeking healing.

"Burke, don't give up on the future. Not now when you have Meggie to consider. The future is full of wonderful possibilities." She pushed aside regret that her future was set by the desires of her loving parents. She would no doubt find it satisfying once she adjusted. "You're a good man, Burke Edwards. Don't forget it."

The hunger in Burke's gaze slowly grew. "You almost make me believe."

"Believe. It's true."

He studied her mouth and lowered his head.

She knew he intended to kiss her. Knew she should back away, refuse it. But he needed the comfort and reassurance a little kiss would give and she lifted her mouth to meet his.

His lips were warm, gentle, questioning.

She leaned into him, his arms at her elbows anchoring her. He tasted of sage and sunshine, strength and adventure. To her shame she clung to him, seeking more.

This was wrong. It took every ounce of self-control, memory of every well-taught lesson to pull away.

His hands on her elbows kept her from fleeing.

She kept her head down, staring at the ground between them as guilt washed through her in waves.

"Jenny?"

She backed away. "I didn't come out here to be kissed." Or to kiss.

"Oh." He grinned. "What did you come for?"

She intended to convince him to reconcile with Flora. That was out. But Meggie's need was still the same. "You need to find someone to care for Meggie."

He caught her arm, his fingers burning through

the fabric of her dress, shredding her resolve. "I have the perfect person in mind."

She knew he meant her and surprise and sorrow intermingled. It would be a good solution for Meggie's needs. It hurt Jenny clear through to contemplate leaving the little girl. She would think no further. She controlled her thoughts so her eyes would reveal nothing. "Good. Who?" She tried to inject a teasing note to her voice and wondered how successful she'd been.

"You." He gently rubbed her arm making it impossible to think clearly.

"Me?" She croaked the word.

"You're perfect for the job. Meggie knows you. You and Paquette get along. Dare I think you even like the prairies? A rare thing indeed."

She couldn't look at him, knowing her hopes showed on her face, naked and raw, aching to be acknowledged. She could not allow them freedom and closed her eyes. *Father God, help me. Give me strength.*

Slowly her world returned to normal and she faced him squarely. "I can't. Ted—"

"Ted." He spat the word out. "Your father's choice." The pain in his eyes almost melted her resolve. "You won't tell me what you want. Or do you even know? Maybe you're too weak to have an opinion. Like I said. This is no country for weak women."

Originally it had been women in general. Then women from the East. Now it was weak women and that's how he saw her. If only he knew how hard it had been for her to learn to be submissive. But that was a story she would never share.

He spun around on his heel. "Forget it. We will manage fine on our own. There are five adults here to help with Meggie. We don't need outsiders."

Burke swung into the saddle and kicked the horse into a gallop. He didn't slow until his mount was lathered and breathing hard and then only to rest the animal. Why had he let himself think Jenny was different? Just because she seemed to enjoy the prairies didn't mean—what? What did he want it to mean? Besides, it wasn't the prairies he wanted her to care about. It wasn't only Meggie he wanted her help with. He wanted her to care about him enough to consider staying, consider making up her own mind about who she would marry.

He touched his lips, remembering how she'd yielded to his kiss. Slowly he smiled. No mistaking her reaction. There was something between them whether or not she admitted it.

He slapped his thigh. Great. Wonderful news. Because it made no difference. She intended to return home to the man of her father's choosing. He couldn't believe it. He'd accused her of being weak but he knew better. Or at least, he thought he did. He'd seen her deal with a cranky Meggie on the train and remain unruffled. He'd watched her help Paquette. Of course, maybe it was only good breeding.

He'd been so angry when he'd seen her with that black rebel of a horse. She could have been killed if the animal struck out with his hooves as he invariably did when any of the men approached him, and yet he'd watched her stroking the animal's head. Maybe it was simply blind good fortune, not courage or perseverance.

He had no solid reason to think she was anything other than a well-trained Easterner. In fact, the more he thought about it, the more convinced he grew that's exactly what she was.

Believing so made it easier to plan to take her back to town and put her on the train to her pa and her Ted.

He'd inform her of his decision tonight.

Regret threatened to suck his insides out.

Maybe he'd wait until tomorrow to give himself time to get used to the idea.

By morning the idea was no more welcome than it had been the day before. He milked the cow, fed the cats and tended to his chores, taking lots of time, delaying his return to the house when he must make the announcement.

Finally he could find no more excuses. He sighed. Knowing what he must do did not make it any easier. He stood outside the barn and stared at the rank horse she'd been petting yesterday. Fragments of her actions dashed across his thoughts. Her head close to the horse's black head, almost touching. The way she lifted her face to the sky and laughed. The sight of her standing several yards from the buildings, gazing into the distance. The touch of her lips on his. He sighed. Those sights and sounds and feelings would be difficult to erase. But he must put them behind him. Never think of her back East with Ted. The name burned a bloody path through his mind.

He shoved a load of determination into his body and ordered his boots to march toward the house. He grabbed the neglected bucket of milk and crossed the yard. Halfway across he heard Meggie wailing and Jenny's soothing tones as she tried to calm her. Meggie hadn't cried like this since the first day or two.

Meggie's cries paused.

Burke relaxed. Only a momentary upset. Nothing to worry about.

He hadn't even completed the thought when Meggie started again, long shuddering sobs filled with shrill anguish.

What was wrong?

He rushed the last few yards, dashed in the door.

Jenny sat on Paquette's chair struggling with Meggie, who tossed her head back and forth.

Burke swung the pail to the cupboard without taking his eyes off the pair. He crossed to squat before them. "Meggie, what's wrong?"

She screamed.

He sought Jenny's gaze. Read her frustration and something else—worry?

"I'm trying to get her clothes on."

Seemed ordinary enough. Shouldn't upset Meggie. He turned his attention to the child. "Come on, sweetie, let Jenny dress you."

Meggie gave him a defiant look without letting up on the racket.

"Give her to me." He plucked Meggie up and struggling to hold her, took the little socks and boots Jenny handled. Impossibly small. He struggled to handle the tiny things and at the same time, corral Meggie. But he would manage. He had to prove to himself and Jenny that they didn't need her.

He caught Meggie's foot.

She wailed and twisted away leaving him with a stocking and no foot.

He snagged her thrashing limb and held on. He could do this…if he had another set of hands.

Jenny yanked the stocking from his tight grip and slipped it on as he held Meggie's foot. Working as a team they managed the other stocking and the little boots. By the time they finished, both were disheveled and sweating. Meggie was a sopping mess of tears.

Jenny wiped her face with a towel. "Honey, what's the matter?"

Meggie screamed.

"This is unacceptable." Burke shifted the baby so she was facing him. It was like trying to corral water. She slipped through his hands every time he thought he had her. Finally, he gave up trying to make her face him and simply held her. "Meggie, behave yourself."

His firm tone made no impression.

"Meggie, stop or I'll put you in your room."

No change.

He marched to the bedroom and sat her on the bed. "You can come out when you're done."

She curled into a ball with her back to him and sobbed.

He could hardly stand it. She sounded so miserable. Made him feel so helpless. How did one deal with a squalling child? No doubt some would suggest a spanking but he couldn't bring himself to do so. She barely knew him, had lost both her parents and been transported halfway across the country. Seems it was enough to drive an adult to tears let alone a child. But how to console her?

He would hold her, rock her. "Meggie, come here." He touched her shoulder.

She curled tighter and wailed louder. "Mama."

The cry made him want to join her. His parents were dead. His sister dead. The woman he intended to marry in an asylum. And he was prepared to send a woman he could see himself growing to love back East to marry another. Meggie's cries reached into the ache of his heart, gave it breath and life. *Oh, Meggie, I know how it hurts.*

Ignoring her resistance, he scooped the baby to his lap and cuddled her close, rocking back and forth. "Hush, little baby, don't you cry. I will sing you a lullaby." He crooned words from some deep forgotten corner of his memories. He didn't even know he knew these words. He must have heard his own mother sing them. Perhaps to him. Or to Lena. His throat tightened so he couldn't go on. The pain of all his losses brought hot tears to the back of his throat.

After a few minutes, Meggie's sobs settled into shuddering gasps. Burke got his own emotions safely relegated to the back rooms of his mind. Along with every speck of feeling toward Jenny. For his sake, his sanity, for all of them, she needed to leave. Before he couldn't let her go.

He and Meggie would do just fine with Paquette to help.

* * *

Jenny heaved a sigh of relief as Burke took Meggie into the bedroom. She'd been at her wit's end to quiet the child. What was wrong with her? Was the reality of her loss making itself felt? If so, they would all be hard-pressed to provide her some measure of comfort.

Burke's voice came to her. First, pleading words and then a song. A lullaby. He was singing to the baby, his voice deep and calming. Plucking at something unfamiliar deep inside.

Drawn by curiosity and an invisible thread that bound her to this pair, she tiptoed to the bedroom and drew to a halt at the doorway.

Burke cradled the baby and crooned, his head bent as if he intended to shelter Meggie from every danger, every hurt.

She reached toward the pair, wanting to add her comfort, share the way they clung to each other. She wanted to hold them both close. Be held close by them. Or perhaps be held by Burke as they closed their arms around Meggie.

This was wrong. How could she yearn after him when she'd given her promise to another?

Why did she continue to find submission so difficult? Had she not learned her lesson? She shuddered. Her eyes stung with shame. Yes, she'd learned the risks of ignoring her parents' wise guidance. They only wanted to protect her even as Burke wanted to protect Meggie. She lifted her fingers as if she could touch the pair and be part of them. Then she spun away, unnoticed by either and returned to the kitchen.

She would leave immediately. In fact, she'd announce her intention at breakfast.

Burke and Meggie would manage well enough without her.

Chapter Eight

Her resolve was firmly in place when Burke entered the room with Meggie in his arms. It faltered only slightly when Burke met her eyes. She imagined regret and longing in his gaze, but knew it was only concern about Meggie. He had no idea of her foolish imaginations. She ducked her head lest her eyes give her away.

Now was the time to act.

She was about to make her announcement when the men trooped in, ready for breakfast.

Burke stepped to her side. Was he going to say something to try and change her mind? She stomped back the little thrill on the heels of the idea. Her mind was made up. He only wanted someone to look after Meggie, but they would manage on their own. Though she wondered how well they'd do.

"Time for breakfast, little Meg peg."

She silently mocked her thoughts. He only wanted to put Meggie in her customary place at Jenny's side.

Meggie stiffened and refused to let go of Burke.

Jenny closed her eyes against the feeling sweeping over her. She could understand Meggie's reluctance to leave those comforting arms.

"I guess you can sit on my knee. Just this once. Remember, Meg peg. This is just once."

He settled in his place and awkwardly tried to fill his plate while struggling to hold a squirming baby. Meggie simply wasn't going to be content. Jenny took pity on him and dug out a generous portion of scrambled eggs to place on his plate.

Thinking Meggie might be hungry, she offered her a taste of Burke's eggs.

Meggie started to cry again.

"I can't imagine what's wrong with her." Jenny studied the fretful little girl.

Paquette made clucking noises. "Child not happy."

That was an understatement if Jenny had ever heard one. But why? Was she sick? Sad? Naughty? Spoiled? She didn't believe the latter. Besides, she was certainly getting her share of attention at the moment.

Burke eyed his plate of food. She could almost feel his mouth watering. Then he sighed. "You eat first,

Jenny. Then maybe she'll settle for you so I can eat."
He pushed from the table and strode outside.

No one spoke as they listened to his boots thudding back and forth on the veranda floor as he sang to Meggie, who settled into a fitful fuss.

"Do you think she's sick?" She meant the question for anyone at the table but directed it at Paquette.

"Not sick. Hurt."

"Hurt? How?" Had she fallen? Been dropped? Had Paquette seen something?

"She be on horse day before." Paquette rubbed her legs and then her neck. "Hard work for baby."

"Ahh." Of course. "Anything we can do for her?"

Paquette mumbled some foreign sounding words. "I make the rub." She finished her meal then left the table and hurried to her room.

Jenny stared after her then slowly turned back to her food.

Mac touched her elbow. "Paquette knows Indian cures."

Jenny nodded though her thoughts weren't easy. Was this something Burke allowed? She cleaned her plate and went to take Meggie from his arms. "Paquette says Meggie is sore from the ride yesterday."

Burke blinked. "I did this to her?"

At the shock and regret in his eyes, she wished she hadn't said anything. "Paquette is making a rub."

"I only meant to make her part of the ranch."

"I'm sure she'll be fine."

"How could I expect her to ride like a man? She's a baby. It was wrong of me." He grunted. "Seems I'm always misjudging the females in my life." His eyes grew hard. He flexed his jaw muscles then spun away and returned to the kitchen.

From the look he'd given her, Jenny knew he included her in his misjudgments though he had no right to do so. She'd been honest from the beginning. She'd told him she would return home and fulfill her promise to Pa to marry Ted. He had no right to ask her to stay.

Did he really think she would?

Her heart begged to be released so she could.

She quieted it.

Adventure was not in her future. Nor was the thrill of sharing life with a man like Burke. Only a long slow obedience. It was for the best. But acknowledging it did nothing to ease the pain threatening to bring her to her knees.

Meggie's pitiful cries anchored her in her responsibilities, her duty. She couldn't leave today. Not with Meggie fussy. It wouldn't be fair to her. Or Paquette. Or Burke.

Nor did she object to the delay.

Her conscience accused her of unkindness that she could be even faintly happy that the situation gave her an excuse to stay another day. After all, Meggie's suffering was responsible for buying her a reprieve.

I'll do everything to help Meggie. It was faint comfort to her guilt.

Burke poked his head out the door. "Paquette is ready." He waited at the door and touched her upper arm as she stepped through. She felt his urgency, knew he sought comfort from his guilt.

"Burke, don't blame yourself. No one guessed this would happen."

"I wouldn't have listened if anyone suggested it. My mind was made up. Well, it's made up again. From now on Meggie stays with Paquette until she's old enough to saddle her own horse. Unless…" He sought her eyes, silently asking her to reconsider her refusal to stay.

"I can't."

"Then let's get on with it."

She didn't know if he meant taking care of Meggie, or her leaving, or both. But she would not allow herself to think beyond her boundaries. She would focus on Meggie.

When she tried to put Meggie down so she could take the bowl of thick paste Paquette handed her, Meggie plunked on her bottom, leaning her head over her lap and crying hard enough to make Jenny want to sob along with her. "I didn't realize her legs hurt too much to stand."

"I'll put her on the bed." Burke scooped her up.

Jenny took the concoction from Paquette.

"Wipe on legs and back. Not get in eyes."

Burke already had Meggie stripped down to her petticoat. They perched on the edge of the bed, gently smoothing the pungent rub as Paquette had instructed. As they worked, they murmured to Meggie, assuring her she'd be feeling better real soon.

After a few minutes, Meggie relaxed and fell asleep.

They remained at her side.

"Poor baby," Burke murmured. "To think I did this to her."

"She'll be fine."

"Will she? She needs a mother."

Jenny couldn't argue. She'd been saying the same thing since her arrival.

He continued. "She had a mother. God saw fit to take her. Makes me even more convinced God is busy with the universe and has no time for petty details of our lives."

"Oh no. God is concerned with details."

"And you base this surety on what?"

She sought for the basis of her conviction. "Have you ever turned a leaf over and studied the intricate pattern? Have you compared leaves from different species of trees and seen how they vary?"

"What's leaves got to do with humans?"

"Think about the birds. How each is so different. The variety of flowers. Why, even the sky. Such a display of color every morning and evening and never the same."

"Yes?" He sounded impatient.

"Do you think a God who specializes in such variety is unconcerned with the details of our lives?"

He shrugged. "Seems to me nature simply repeats itself. Hardly proves a thing." He fixed her with a demanding stare. "Tell me of a time when you knew beyond a shadow of a doubt that God cared about the details of your life."

She didn't doubt God cared even about little things in her life, but she knew she also had choices to make. She wasn't sure how to reconcile the two. Too often her choices seemed to bring dire consequences. But she could hardly blame God for them.

"What brings that little frown to your forehead?"

She quickly forced her muscles to relax.

"Do you have doubts you aren't willing to admit?"

"My doubts are regarding my own ability to do the right thing. I have no doubts about God's sure hand."

"Ahh. Now I see."

"What?"

"Why you allow your father to choose your

husband. You are afraid to take responsibility for the choice." He leaned closer, his eyes dark and demanding. "You're afraid to be who you were meant to be."

She snorted but couldn't find a response, afraid of where her natural instincts led her. "I have reason to be cautious."

"Is it caution or are you hiding? They're different. I think—"

She didn't want to hear what he thought and half rose.

He caught her hand and stopped her, pulling her close until she practically bumped into his legs. Heat flared up her neck, and she dropped back to the edge of the bed rather than deal with such intimate closeness.

"I think the things you desire frighten you because they go against the constraints of your Eastern society."

She wanted to deny it, but how could she when she struggled with the very thing every day? But she wouldn't let him guess how correct he was. "Yeah. Like what?"

He leaned back, pleased with himself, as if he knew he had struck close to home. "Like adventure. Challenge. Risk. I think I have to amend my opinion."

She couldn't tear herself away from his amused, probing stare.

"Perhaps there are women who belong in this country."

"You mean apart from the ones bred and born out here?" She couldn't keep the sarcasm from her voice. Didn't want to. Wanted to use it to stop him before he went further, probing into territory forbidden to everyone, including herself.

His expression shifted and grew distant.

Instantly she regretted her sarcasm. Wanted to pull the words back and return to that challenging, tempting place of a few minutes ago.

"However, we both know you won't admit what you really want. Jenny, what happened to make you so scared of who you are?"

She opened her mouth to deny anything had happened. The words wouldn't come. Because they'd be false. Something had happened. Something she couldn't undo. But never again would she listen to that inner voice calling for adventure. *Lord God, my heavenly Father, help me remember how dangerous that inner voice is. Help me hear Your voice guiding and protecting me.* The voice she heard came from scriptures she had memorized. One had become her motto. 'Honor thy father and thy mother that thy days may be long upon the land which the Lord thy God giveth thee.'

"Jenny, are you pretending you can't see me? Can't hear me?"

She realized she sat with her eyes closed and opened them. Forced herself to meet his gaze. Her heart cracked at the concern she saw. Quickly, she patched the crack and smiled, knowing it probably looked as false as it felt. "I see you just fine."

"You aren't going to tell me what happened, are you?"

"Not ever."

He chuckled. "At least now I know for sure something did."

She heaved out hot frustrated air. She'd revealed more than she wanted. But it didn't change anything. Her secret would never be revealed. "It doesn't take two of us to sit with Meggie. Do you want me to stay with her?"

"I'll stay. After all, this is my fault."

"Fine. I'll go help Paquette."

"Jenny?" He reached for her.

But she slipped away. There was nothing either of them could say to change the reality of their situation. She would stay another day or two—only as long as it took for Meggie to recover. And then she would return home.

* * *

Burke watched her leave, wishing things could be different. He said she might be the sort of woman to live here. It was only wishful thinking on his part. She belonged no more than Flora, though he knew she wouldn't likely end up in an asylum. What had quenched her vivid spirit he'd glimpsed at unguarded moments? He tried to convince himself it didn't matter. But he longed to know, longed to see her enjoy life to the fullest.

Did God care about such details?

His mother seemed to think so. As did Jenny. But so far, he'd managed quite well without God's help.

Or had he?

Would God have changed things for Flora if he asked? He hadn't, but almost certainly her parents had, so the answer was probably not.

But could he manage to raise Meggie without making mistakes? Big mistakes that would create calamity? Maybe he needed God's help in that area, though he wasn't sure how he could expect to see it. How would he know if God did intervene in some way? Could he ask for something specific—sort of a test?

He didn't like the idea one bit. It felt like challenging God, which he wasn't about to do. Guess he'd just continue as he had been doing. Managing on his own as best he could, accepting the consequence of his mistakes, hoping to learn from them and do better in the future.

Meggie wakened and cried. Jenny hurried in. "Paquette says to smear her again."

He welcomed Jenny's help caring for Meggie. Wished he could have it into the foreseeable future. But no point in wanting things he couldn't have.

But if it didn't feel so wrong he would almost be glad Meggie's pain had given him reason enough to put off telling Jenny it was time to leave.

But he couldn't put it off forever.

Knowing the time would come far too soon, pain drove cruel fingers through his gut.

By evening Meggie seemed better, though she still refused to walk so he hung about, carrying her from place to place.

She did allow him to seat her at Jenny's side for supper and she ate a small amount.

While Paquette and Jenny cleaned the kitchen Burke took Meggie outside. He hoped Jenny would go for their customary evening walk even though she'd been cool and businesslike since their morning conversation.

Paquette came out first, a buckskin bag hung over her shoulder, and headed off across the prairies without a backward look.

He watched her.

"She says she's going to find more healing plants."

He hadn't noticed Jenny coming out and jerked around at her voice. She stood framed in the doorway, the sun pooling in her features and bathing her in a golden glow. She looked as if she'd been kissed by sunlight. His heart drank in the sight, letting it drench every corner, revealing secrets hidden in the dark.

He wanted to share his life with her.

He swallowed hard. It wasn't possible. She had promised to marry another even though he suspected she didn't love this Ted fellow. To please her pa. Or was it because she didn't want to admit to being the person she truly was?

The woman created by God.

One thought triggered another in rapid succession.

If she was running from who she was, wasn't she running from God? And would God see fit to intervene if that was the case?

He didn't know. But somehow it felt as if God was on his side. He held the thought carefully, wishing he had time to examine it more closely.

Perhaps, in this case, it was fine to ask God to listen to his prayer. *God, you know my doubts, my uncertainties. But this one thing I'm certain of. Jenny is hiding from something. Show her how to deal with it. Help her.*

He wanted to ask for more. For Jenny to be willing to stay on the ranch. To help with Meggie. To stay for him.

But he couldn't ask for all that. It was too selfish.

"Ready for our walk?" he asked.

She quirked an eyebrow as if to ask when it had become "our walk." Then she nodded. "I could use some fresh air."

Meggie rested happily in his arms as they headed for the barn. She sat on the floor as mama cat greeted her but insisted on being carried again as they went to see the horses. He held her as she touched each muzzle and giggled.

Then they headed for the open prairie.

Sure she needed fresh air. However, she didn't need to accompany Burke to get it. But for the life of her she couldn't refuse the opportunity even though she'd been angry with him for poking at her deepest feelings. How often had she wondered why God made her a woman bound by the constraints of her society? She looked about the rolling grassland. Out here, the boundaries were different—pushed back like the horizon was. Perhaps if she'd met Burke earlier….

There she went again, chasing after dreams, ignoring her parents' wise counsel. She reined in her feelings. She would not be making that mistake again.

Some persistent voice whispered, "How is Burke a mistake?" The mistake was in thinking this visit could be anything more than that—a visit with a task to do.

Meggie babbled away contentedly in Burke's arms.

Jenny wondered if Meggie's legs still hurt or if she was enjoying the attention so much she intended to pretend they did. Not that she could blame the little girl. And if it meant Meggie and Burke grew closer, well, all the better.

She sought for something to talk about that would take her mind from these wayward travels. "Is there church in Buffalo Hollow?"

"Not that I know of. Why?"

"Nothing's been said. I've seen no sign of anyone attending. So I wondered. Lena would surely want Meggie raised to go to church."

Burke sighed. "I expect that's so."

"But?"

"I hadn't thought about the necessity. Didn't seem important until now."

She chuckled, knowing he'd likely given the whole idea little if any thought. "Would you have gone even if there was a church?"

He gave her a mocking grin. "You have come to know me too well, I fear."

The thought burned through her careful self-control. Did she know him? Not as well as she wanted. She tried to think of Ted. Did she know him any better? She had no idea how he felt about God. Did he go to church out of habit or conviction? Had he faced troubles? If he had—or when he did— what would his reaction be? Would he be like Burke and say it proved God wasn't interested in details of human existence? She'd never asked him any of these questions. In fact, they had never discussed anything but daily occurrences—how many people had come into the store, the pleasure of the new shipment— mundane stuff about his business interests. She knew practically nothing about Ted and had absolutely no curiosity about him. How odd when her heart yearned to peel back every layer of Burke's thinking until she saw the pulsing core of his thoughts.

She realized he watched her with a bemused expression, as if aware she'd done a mental side trip. It required a great effort to bring herself back. "So would you have gone?" She guessed he might have with Flora's urging but not otherwise.

"I would have considered it when Flora was here."

She laughed, pleased she had guessed correctly. "And never before or since. Funny, I thought that might be your answer."

He shifted Meggie to one arm and caught her

hand. "I might see the value of attending if I had someone to go with me."

He was asking again for her to stay. Using his need to go to church as an incentive. Her thoughts ran away like wild horses turned free. She imagined sitting beside him in a church, singing together, worshipping together. It held appeal like she'd never before felt at church attendance. The skin across her cheeks shrank as guilt flared up her throat. She'd let her willful spirit turn worship into a—she swallowed hard—a romantic event. God forgive her. "I guess you'll see what can be done to start services so you can attend, seeing as you have someone to go with."

Hope flared in his eyes. "I do?"

She couldn't pull from the warmth in his eyes even though she knew it was wrong. His dark gaze seemed to seek and find secrets in her heart. Secrets she longed to share with someone who wouldn't consider them scandalous. But they were. Furthermore, even her present thinking was wrong and shameful. She had promised to marry another. Yes, of her parents' choosing, but she trusted her parents, knew they understood her, cared only about what was best for her. They'd seen where her rebellious spirit led and had protected her from the damage she might have incurred.

Her fingers cramped. She realized she curled her hands into tight fists and used the pain to fuel her resolve. "You have Meggie to go to church with you."

Disappointment flared through his eyes. His smile flattened and his cheeks appeared wooden. "I see you're still running."

His assessment stung. "I am making what I consider to be a wise decision."

He snorted—a sound ripe with mockery. "Wise or safe? Or is it fear that makes you cling to what your father decides for you?"

She breathed so hard she wondered if her nostrils flared. "I am not afraid of anything. Never have been. Never will be."

"Then why are you prepared to return home to marry a man you don't love?"

He touched her arm so gently she couldn't pull away, couldn't deny herself the comfort his touch brought, melting away, as it did, her anger and fear. Yes, she feared where her own desires would lead her but at this moment, with his fingers warming her elbow and his eyes kind and pleading, none of that mattered.

"Jenny, tell me you don't feel a little excitement at the idea of being part of building something solid in this new land. Then I will believe you don't secretly long to stay here." His voice lowered and he brushed his hand up to her shoulder. She thought he meant to kiss her by the way he looked at her. She couldn't think past her longing for him to do so.

But he waited.

She realized he expected her to say something but couldn't, for the life of her, remember what they'd been talking about. All she could think was how nothing else mattered but being here with Burke, Meggie safely sheltered in his arm. It would take only one step for her to be as safely sheltered in his other arm.

"No," she wailed. She would not allow it to happen. Not again would she allow her emotions or her longings to control her actions. "This is all wrong." She fled back to the house, remembering only after she stood panting inside the kitchen that she had to put Meggie to bed.

She struggled with her thoughts. She knew what was right for her. Being here threatened that. As soon as Meggie felt better she would be leaving. A trickle of guilt pulled at her conscience. Paquette was not able to deal with an active two-year-old. However, that was not her concern. It was Burke's.

But what about her promise to Lena?

Surely, Lena would understand she'd done the best she could. Her resolve firmly under control, she put on her most calm face and turned to face Burke as he stepped through the door. She moved to take Meggie. "It's time for this little one to go to bed."

Meggie protested weakly at the idea then came to Jenny arms.

"Good night." She waited for him to leave.

He hesitated, correctly reading the dismissal in her face. She wasn't prepared to discuss this any further. "Very well. If that's how you want it. Just think about what you're giving up."

She quirked an eyebrow questioningly before she could stop herself and pretend she didn't wonder exactly what he meant. Before he could respond she headed for the bedroom. She tried but failed to stop her thoughts from making a list of what she was giving up—the open prairie, the sense of adventure, a chance to conquer the land as he'd said. All of those things paled in comparison to the knowledge she would give up a chance to share her life with Burke. Not that he had exactly said that. He wanted someone to help with Meggie. That's all. She needed to keep the truth clearly before her.

She didn't love him. She couldn't. As she prepared Meggie for bed, she prayed. *Father God, keep me pure and true. Strengthen my resolve.*

Meggie fell asleep almost immediately and Jenny returned to the kitchen. Paquette had not come back and she used the chance to write another letter home. She had to fill the pages without revealing the truth of her heart—that she cared for Burke far more than she should. So she described the prairie.

I want to laugh with joy when I see the wind ripple the grass. And the sunsets and sunrises are so beautiful they make my heart glad. It's a bold, new land that requires strong people. The men are adventuresome. I've met few women but the ones I have seem full of grit and good humor. It makes me want to get to know them better.

She went on to describe how Meggie was doing.

Burke took her for a long horseback ride yesterday and we are all paying for it today. She is very sore. Paquette mixed up some native ointment that seemed to relieve her suffering. Meggie is sleeping now.

I wonder how she will do when I leave. A two-year-old needs so much attention.

Should she explain Paquette would be helping Burke? She could see no reason not to do so.

Burke expects Paquette to care for Meggie while he is out. I try not to worry how it will work. As soon as I am reasonably happy with the situation in regards to Meggie's care I will return home as promised.

She closed a few lines later and sealed the letter, ready to be taken to town the next time someone went.

A glance out the window revealed it was almost dark. Paquette was not yet back. Of course she would be fine. As Burke said, she was born here. Could probably find her way home blindfolded. But for her peace of mind, Jenny decided to wait up until the older woman was safely back home.

Chapter Nine

Jenny stared out into the night. A lamp glowed from the bunkhouse window, an echo of the lamp on the table behind her. Otherwise, the prairie was dark and silent.

Several times she'd gone to the veranda and listened. Apart from the evening rustle of the horses settling down and the gentle lowing of the milk cow, the only sound was the far–off yipping of coyotes. She strained to hear something indicating that Paquette had made her way back.

Nothing.

Jenny's neck tingled. She couldn't shake her tension. Didn't know if she should be worried or not.

She turned from the window and walked to the bedroom. Meggie slept. On the off chance Paquette had slipped in unnoticed—and Jenny knew it was impossible—she peeked into Paquette's room. The narrow, fur-covered cot was empty. She glanced around the room, noting the herbs hanging from the rafters, the little baskets lining a shelf. She smiled. It looked and smelled like Paquette—a comforting presence.

Where was the woman? How long did she wait before she notified Burke?

She returned to staring out the window, feeling alone and abandoned. Burke and the men were only a few yards away, yet were totally unaware of the situation.

Her heart squeezed out a flood of worry. Surely Paquette should be back by now. Something must have happened. She refused to think of what that "something" might be.

She checked again to make sure Meggie slept soundly then obeyed her instincts and marched over to the bunkhouse. The sound of laughter and deep voices came from inside; she heard the creak of wood, like someone tipping a chair or—she swallowed hard, knowing she approached forbidden territory. Forbidden or not, she must talk to Burke. She rapped on the door. Instant silence greeted her knock.

She called, "It's me, Jenny. I need to talk to Burke."

Lots of shuffling and whispering ensued and then the light shifted. It reappeared when the door opened, held in Burke's hand.

"You need me?"

Was she crazy or did she hear a welcome longing in his voice? Now was not the time to let her emotions take over. "It's Paquette."

Burke's expression shifted through a range of emotions—surprise, disappointment and then concern. "What's wrong?"

"She's not back. I don't know if I should be worried or not. But I thought you should be the one to decide." The words came like a bolt of lightning. She didn't realize until she spoke just how concerned she was. "Should she be out this late? Is she safe out there after dark? What if something has happened to her?"

"Whoa. Slow down." He gripped her shoulder.

His touch calmed her. He would know what to do.

He turned to the men. "Boys, we need to find Paquette."

"Aww, boss. I'm tired," Dug moaned but grunted as if getting to his feet. From the thumping inside the bunkhouse, she guessed they all pulled on boots.

"Meet me at the veranda. Bring me a horse." Burke took Jenny's hand and led her to the house. "You need to stay here with Meggie. If Paquette returns before we do, I need you to signal us."

"How will I do that?"

He pulled a rifle from the cupboard. "Fire this

off, three shots about fifteen seconds apart. Do you know how to shoot this?"

"I've never even touched a gun."

He showed her how to load it and pull the trigger. "Most important thing—press it hard to your shoulder and brace yourself for the kick. Oh, and aim at the sky. I wouldn't want you killing one of the horses or blowing a hole through the bunkhouse."

Her giggle revealed her nervousness.

He looked at her with narrowed eyes. "You'll be able to do this?"

She tipped her chin upward. "Of course." In fact, it was exciting to contemplate. Who'd believe she might get a chance to fire a real gun? Pa would be—well, she didn't know if he'd be shocked or surprised or what. "I'll be fine. Go find Paquette and, Burke, God be with you and help you find her safe and sound."

"You really believe God will help?"

"I certainly do. I pray He will give you eyes to see and ears to hear."

He squeezed her hand. "You pray and we'll look."

The men rode up to the door, leading a horse for Burke. They all carried lanterns and handed one to Burke as he mounted. He ordered the men in different directions. Just before he rode away, he turned and nodded to Jenny as if they shared something special.

Perhaps they did. A shared concern over Paquette. An agreement to pray.

And something more. Something tenuous and forbidden but real. For tonight she was glad to acknowledge at least a fraction of her feelings for him—her confidence in his ability to find Paquette and a certainty that he trusted her to pray.

Burke hoped Jenny hadn't guessed how concerned he was over Paquette's absence. It wasn't unusual for her to wander the prairie but she always returned by dark. She knew better than most the dangers of being out after that. How easily one could get turned around if the stars and moon were hidden as they were tonight. The danger of tripping in a gopher hole, falling and breaking something.

Finding her in the dark required a miracle. Why, they might ride three feet from her and if she couldn't call out...well they would miss her as much as if she were ten miles away.

Jenny said God would help. He wasn't sure he believed it, but she seemed to believe enough for both of them.

He rode slowly, pausing often to call and listen. He heard the men doing the same thing. "Paquette!" The sound echoed across the land, the only answer the whir of birds' wings as they startled from their sleep.

His search took him farther and farther away from the ranch and with every step, his worry grew. Where was she? How could he hope to find her in this pitch-black night?

The darkness and the light are both alike to thee.

The words came softly from some distant room of his memories. He remembered his mother saying the words. They were from the Bible.

He didn't doubt God saw as well in the dark as in the light. But would He allow Burke the same ability? Or at least guide him to Paquette? Jenny seemed to think He would. He certainly needed help beyond human ability. Now might be a good time to forget his doubts and believe in God's divine help.

Lord God, you made the universe. You made night and day. They are the same to You. You know I have trouble believing You bother with the numerous details of mankind but if You do, please be so kind as to show me where Paquette is.

It was a weak sort of prayer yet the first real one he'd offered in too many years to count and it felt good. As if he'd turned from showing his back to God, to showing his face. Whether or not it would make a difference…well, time would tell.

He continued on. Riding a few feet, stopping, calling and listening. Nothing. His doubts returned. Seems God couldn't be bothered with man's many problems.

He got off his horse. Couldn't explain why he did. Wasn't like he was tired of riding. Shoot, he could ride all night if he wanted. He waved the lantern around more out of desperation than hope. Saw nothing and lowered the light. Something on the ground caught his eye. A flash of something bright. He plucked it up. A bead necklace. Like the ones Paquette wore. He straightened and turned again, the light above his head. Did he detect a movement on the edge of the patch of light? He stepped closer. This time he was sure a shadow shifted. Two more steps and he made out a shape. "Paquette, what are you doing?"

She didn't move, her only response a soft mutter.

His nerves tensed. "Paquette?"

She shifted as if startled. Lifted her head then wilted and resumed her mumbling.

He strode over, shining the light in her face. "Paquette, are you hurt?"

She acted as if she hadn't heard.

He touched her shoulder, felt the chill of her body. "Come on, let's go home." He urged her to her feet. She hadn't walked upright since he'd met her, but she seemed to have curled closer to the ground, her steps agonizingly slow. He didn't ask her any more questions. All that mattered at the moment was getting her home.

Ignoring her mumbled protests, he lifted her to the saddle and swung up to ride behind her. Several times she swayed. Only his arms around her kept her from pitching headlong to the ground.

She'd be fine as soon as she got back to the shelter of the house, as soon as she got warm. He had to believe it. But his nerves twitched with worry. Paquette was quiet and withdrawn. Flora had been loud and aggressive. Still the similarities stunned him. Seems this land was too much, even for those bred and born in it. He would do well to remember. Expecting any woman to settle here and survive the challenges was not reasonable. He quietly and firmly pushed aside the picture of Jenny in his kitchen every day for the rest of his life. It simply wasn't possible. It would eventually destroy her, and he couldn't bear for that to happen.

He concentrated on getting Paquette back to the house. "Jenny, I found her."

Jenny was already racing across the veranda, alerted by the hoofbeats of his horse.

He swung down, catching Paquette in his arms as he touched the ground.

"Is she hurt?"

"I don't know. She's cold though."

Jenny rushed back inside, calling over her shoulder. "Bring her in and I'll tend her."

He was hot on her heels. As she ran for a blanket, he dragged a chair out with his boot and deposited Paquette. She slumped forward.

Jenny returned and wrapped her warmly. She rubbed Paquette's hands. "Are you hurt? Did you fall?"

Paquette stopped mumbling, slowly lifted her head and stared into Jenny's eyes as if searching for answers.

Burke's heart beat loudly against his chest. This was so unlike Paquette. The woman had fought for survival after being abandoned on the prairie. To see her so small and weak…

Paquette shook her head. "Not remember."

"I'll make some tea." Burke filled the kettle and while he waited for it to boil, took out the teapot and tossed in a handful of tea leaves.

Paquette rocked and mumbled. Several times Jenny caught the blanket as it fell from Paquette's shoulders and rewrapped her.

As soon as the water had any color, he poured a cup of tea and laced it with sugar. He knelt at Jenny's side and held the cup to Paquette's lips.

She stared at him, a look of such confusion in her eyes that he sat back, the tea momentarily forgotten. "Paquette, do you know where you are?"

She glanced around. "Dis not 'ome. My 'ome gone. Gone."

He slanted a look at Jenny. Saw his worry reflected in her eyes. Paquette had lived here three years. This was her home. Yet she seemed to have retreated to an earlier time. "I wonder if she fell."

"Do you hurt anywhere?"

Paquette blinked as if she didn't understand.

Jenny gently ran her hands over Paquette, checking her limbs, feeling her scalp. "She seems uninjured." She again knelt and faced Paquette, studying her face. "Do you know who we are?"

Paquette studied first one then the other. Burke felt as if her gaze reached far into his heart and found nothing she could connect with.

"Maybe I see you afore."

He remembered the cooling tea and held the cup to her lips, urging her to drink.

"I'll help her into bed," Jenny said. "Chances are she'll feel better in the morning."

"Right."

He stepped outside and signaled the men then plunked to a chair and waited, listening to Jenny's soothing tones. He stayed until Jenny returned. "How is she?"

"She seemed glad to see her bed. I'll check her through the night just to make sure. What do you think happened?"

"She must have banged her head somehow." It was an easier answer to swallow than to contemplate that she'd lost more than her way out on the prairie.

He rose and found two mugs. The tea was now

strong enough to use as dye, and he poured in more water before he filled the cups and carried them to the table.

"Thanks." To her credit she didn't grimace when she tasted the strong brew. But perhaps she didn't notice as she stared down the hall.

He was worried about Paquette, too. "She's tough. Likely she'll be fine by morning."

Horses approached the yard. One by one the men stuck their head in the door to ask after Paquette. "She's home safe and is sleeping," Burke told each in turn.

When the last had made an appearance, he and Jenny continued to sit side by side.

"Tell me how you found her."

"Almost didn't. I was only a few feet from her, calling her name but she didn't answer. Should have known then something was wrong with her."

"God certainly guided you tonight."

He'd forgotten his prayer. "Maybe He did. I thought we'd look all night without finding her so I—" He turned so he could see her better, observe her reaction. "I prayed. Sort of a doubters' prayer but I asked for help and not more than a few minutes later, I found her." He recalled the events, telling her every detail—how he'd gotten off the horse, seen the beads, noticed a flicker of movement. "Did God do that?"

She reached for his hand and squeezed. "You know He did, don't you?"

With her warm touch and gentle smile he could believe anything. "Guess so."

She chuckled. "I know it's hard for you to admit you might need to change your mind, but I think you know as well as I that God guided you to her. I think if you allow yourself to believe, you'll see Him at work in many areas of your life."

"I guess God helps in emergencies." He still couldn't believe God cared about everyday, ordinary things.

"'If then God so clothe the grass, which is to day in the field, and tomorrow is cast into the oven; how much more will he clothe you, O ye of little faith?' How much more basic can we get than clothes and food?"

He recognized the Bible verse. Another his mother had quoted often. "Says nothing about food."

She chuckled. "But if I remember correctly, it does in the verse before that. Another verse says He has the hairs of our head numbered. He cares about us. He loves us."

His heart yearned to believe wholly and simply as he had as a child. But life wasn't simple. Nor did it seem to be whole. "What about Lena dying? Did He care about that? Or Flora. Did He do anything about that?" His questions sounded soulful, as if he wanted everything to be fixed, put back to his ideal. It couldn't be. A man simply had to make the best of things, roll with what life dealt.

She continued to hold his hand and without thinking what he did, he turned his palm to hers and interlocked their fingers.

"I can't explain why bad things happen," she said. "Maybe I don't want to. If I understood all the intricacies of life, the end from the beginning, the purpose of pain and suffering, why I think I'd be overwhelmed. I prefer to leave that in God's hands. He is all-wise, all-knowing and all-love. I choose to simply trust Him."

"You make it sound simple."

"In some ways it is."

He wanted to believe, yet at the same time wanted to challenge her because he was certain there were areas where she didn't find trust any easier than he did. "Is it trust or fear that makes you let your father choose the direction of your life—pick your future husband?" He wanted her to confess it was fear and then choose to trust God enough to decide she needed and deserved a man who would honor her strengths. He wanted to be the one she chose, but even if she did that desire must be denied. As soon as Paquette felt better he would send her away—back to safety and sanity.

She twisted her hand away and wrapped her fingers

together in her lap to sit with her head bowed. "It is obedience. God says we are to honor our parents. I have learned to my disgrace the result of not listening to their counsel."

Another hint of having done something she regretted, something making her fearful of following her strong nature. "I don't know what horrible thing you think you did. Maybe someday you'll tell me." It couldn't be as bad as she thought. He captured a bit of hair that had escaped its bounds and played with it. "You are a strong–natured young woman who can boldly face risks and challenges. Yet you intend to pretend you are a docile woman content to follow the lead of your father and then, I suppose, this man you intend to marry. Jenny, I fear you will live a life of regret, always wishing you'd taken the riskier path, the one that led to adventure and—" He couldn't finish. Couldn't say what was in his heart.

He released the bit of hair, curled his fingers over his thumbs and squeezed until his knuckles protested. She would not be at his side. He would not allow it. Far better to know she was safe with another man than to see her spirit slowly die right before his eyes.

Jenny kept her gaze on her hands twisting in her lap. She'd never tell him what happened. Never confess it to anyone. It would remain tucked into a corner of her thoughts. But the idea of being part of this great adventure warred with her determination. Her control was further threatened by the way his fingers brushed her neck as he played with a strand of her hair. Only once before had a man touched her. And that had been so unexpected she hadn't known what to do. It had ended frighteningly. She shuddered at the memory and jerked to her feet. "I'd like to check on Paquette then go to bed, if you don't mind."

He nodded. "Sorry to be a bother." He strode out without a backward look.

She hadn't meant to sound rude or dismissive, but she knew the risks of forgetting her upbringing.

She had difficulty falling asleep as memories twisted through her head, intermingling with worry about Paquette and wishes for things she could never have. Three times she rose and checked on Paquette, who jerked her head up and grumbled at being disturbed.

The morning sun woke her, assisted by Meggie jabbing fingers in Jenny's eyes.

Groaning, she sat up. She'd overslept. No sounds came from the kitchen. Was Paquette not up? She scrambled into her clothes, dressed Meggie hurriedly and let the child run ahead, her sore legs thankfully a thing of the past.

The kitchen echoed with quiet. "Wait here, Meg, while I check on Paquette." She tiptoed to the bedroom. Paquette curled in a ball snoring softly. Poor woman was tired. She'd let her sleep.

That left her to make breakfast for them all. She rubbed her hands in glee. An adventure.

Meggie seemed to remember her sore legs and whined.

Jenny settled her on the floor and handed her some pots and pans to play with while she cooked. A few minutes later she banged the iron bar, smiling at how it had been secured with a piece of stout wire nailed into place with a six-inch spike. Burke wanted to make sure she didn't send it flying in his direction again.

Her thoughts stuttered. She would miss all this when she left. She would miss the prairie, the big kitchen, ringing the bell…and Burke.

The men trooped in for breakfast.

"Where's Paquette?" Burke asked. "She's not—?"

"She's sleeping peacefully. No need to disturb her."

He took in the food she prepared. "You did this by yourself?"

"I did." Satisfaction made her words strong and round.

"And enjoyed it, I venture to say." His eyes spoke approval and something more—a silent challenge.

She nodded. "It was fun."

"As life should be, don't you think?"

His statement was reasonable enough, but she knew he referred to his argument of last night. He seemed to think she was running from things she would enjoy. Well, she was, knowing where such wild abandon, such reckless seeking after adventure led. Why had God made her thus? Or was it only temptation seeking to lead her into dangerous territory? Likely a bit of both, she thought.

His eyes narrowed and she realized she'd allowed him to see too much. He scooped Meggie off the floor and tickled her then put her beside him.

Jenny placed the heaping serving dishes on the table then sat in her customary place. She waited for someone to choose to say the grace, felt a flash of surprise when, without any prodding from the men, Burke announced he would.

He thanked the good Lord for Paquette's safe return and for good food for their hunger. "And thank you Jenny is here, capable of making us a great meal. Amen."

She couldn't look up for fear he would see how his gratitude pleased her. She only did a job that needed doing. Yet it had been a challenge to get everything cooked and ready at the same time and in quantities large enough for the huge appetites of these men. She'd embraced the challenge. It had been fun.

She wouldn't get to do such things when she

returned home. No doubt Ted would hire a house-keeper when they got married. Jenny would be expected to entertain, perhaps be allowed to grow flowers, might occasionally help in the store, though she expected Ted shared Pa's opinion that women belonged in the home. How she would manage to keep boredom at bay she couldn't imagine, but Ma seemed to do so. She would likewise learn how.

But until then, she could enjoy this chance to expand her world.

The men left. Jenny did the dishes before Paquette staggered out, her clothes askew, half her hair hanging in her usual braid and the other half out as if she'd gotten sidetracked before she finished.

"Good morning. How are you feeling?"

Paquette ground to a halt beside Meggie, who had returned to playing on the floor. "Where baby come from?"

Alarm skittered up Jenny's arms. "This is Burke's niece, Meggie. We've been here for days, Paquette. Don't you remember?"

"Not see before. Not know you. Where I am?"

She allowed Jenny to lead her to her chair. "I'll get you coffee and breakfast."

The older woman hunched over as if life had become too heavy to bear.

Jenny served her then played with Meggie so she could unobtrusively observe Paquette.

At first the woman stared at the food then picked at the bacon, but she eventually cleaned her plate and had two cups of black coffee—her usual morning routine.

Jenny eased out a sigh. Whatever had happened would right itself in time. She had to believe that. So why then did she feel a tiny trickle of excitement that for now, she had no choice but to stay and run the kitchen?

She made dinner while Paquette remained at the table, muttering from time to time or letting out long sighs. Other than that, she seemed unaware Jenny did the work she usually did, often refusing Jenny's assistance.

Burke smiled when the men came in to eat. "I see you're up and about, Paquette. You gave us all quite a scare when you didn't come home last night. What happened out there?"

"'Appen? Where?" She looked about as if he meant someone else.

Burke shot Jenny a questioning look. Jenny shook her head. He turned back to Paquette, who examined a spoon as if she had never seen one before.

As they ate, the men tried to engage Paquette in conversation, but she either didn't hear them or acted surprised that they should address her.

Burke waited until the meal was over. "Can I speak to you outside?" he murmured to Jenny.

"Of course." She glanced toward Meggie.

"I'll watch her," Mac offered.

"Thank you," Jenny and Burke said at the same time. Jenny giggled. *Great minds think alike.*

They crossed the veranda and walked toward the corrals. Ebony whinnied a greeting but Burke steered her away from that particular pen. "He's dangerous. Stay away from him."

She thought it wise to omit telling him she visited him every day and had some very interesting discussions with the animal who proved to be an excellent listener.

They wandered to what she would always think of as their favorite place—the end of the trail that ran alongside the corrals until it disappeared into the open prairie.

He didn't mention the subject she knew was uppermost in both their minds until they came to a halt staring out at the blue-gray land under an endless, cloudless cornflower sky. "I'm worried about Paquette. If only there was a doctor nearby."

"I'm sure she'll be fine in a few hours."

He studied her, a slow smile lifting his lips. "Hoping is not the same as being sure."

She lifted one shoulder. "How can I be sure?"

"Have you prayed?"

"No."

"I thought you would have. This is surely one of those times when God needs to intervene."

"Of course." To her shame she hadn't prayed because she knew she had to stay as long as Paquette was so confused. It was a selfish, unchristian attitude. "I certainly will pray for her to get better."

He squeezed her hand. "Me, too."

A great ache engulfed her. His confession connected her to him in a way she didn't want to acknowledge but couldn't deny. If only she could stay here in this very spot and ignore the realities of her life. She couldn't. Right now Meggie needed her, the kitchen needed cleaning—all excuses allowing her to ignore the silent cries of her heart. She wished for a reason to make it impossible to ever leave.

"I better get back." She should pull her hand from his but when he started back, still holding it tight, she made no effort to slip from his grasp. After all, they were both worried about Paquette.

What harm was there in letting herself enjoy comfort and encouragement from his touch?

Chapter Ten

Burke reluctantly, determinedly, released Jenny's hand as they reached the house. He had to make arrangements for her to leave. Somehow they would manage without her. They must. For her sake. "I'm sending Dug to town for supplies. Is there anything you need?"

"I have letters to post. Paquette needed a few things. I'll make a list."

This was an opportune time. For a heartbeat he thought of telling her to prepare to accompany Dug. It was on his mind to say the words but something entirely different came from his mouth. "Do you mind staying until Paquette is better?" He couldn't deny himself this reprieve. Besides, the truth was Paquette could not care for Meggie in her present condition.

Her eyes flared with what he supposed was

surprise. "Of course I will. Someone must care for Meggie." She held his gaze.

He felt her searching deep inside his thoughts, though he couldn't guess what she hoped to find.

Then, even though she didn't move, she withdrew.

Disappointment seared his lungs, making his breath burn his lips in passing. It served to remind him of his intention—not to persuade her to stay but to see she left as soon as possible.

Over the next few days he watched Paquette closely. Often he caught her sitting at the table doing nothing, or perched on a chair on the veranda staring blankly into the distance. What happened out there to change her? Was her state permanent?

He closed his eyes against the treacherous note of gladness that until Paquette was better, Jenny had agreed to stay. It was wrong thinking on his part. He knew it. And his guilt drove him to Paquette's side where she sat on the veranda. "Paquette, how are you?"

"Fine." A bowl of beads sat in her lap, and she sifted them through her fingers.

He turned so he could look in her eyes. Did he catch a flicker of sanity before she ducked away?

She scooped up a handful of beads and let them trickle to the bowl. "Pretty."

Meggie ran outside. She noticed the bowl of beads and leaned over Paquette's knee. "Pretty."

Burke studied the pair. Was he suddenly responsible for two people unable to care for themselves? So long as Jenny was here it wasn't a problem. But Jenny didn't intend to stay.

He didn't intend to let her.

As if his thoughts had beckoned her, she stepped outside and, seeing the three of them together, smiled. "What's so interesting over there?"

"Beads."

"Ah. Paquette enjoys her beads, don't you, Paquette?" She joined them and stroked Paquette's head.

Again, Burke wondered if he detected a flash of something alert in Paquette's eyes, and then she leaned over and mumbled some unfamiliar-sounding words.

Meggie picked a bead from the bowl and popped it into her mouth.

Jenny jerked forward. "No, Meggie. Spit it out." She held out her palm and waited for Meggie to obey. As she straightened, she met Burke's eyes. Paquette should have stopped Meg from putting a bead in her mouth.

Burke gave an acknowledging tilt of his head. Paquette could not be left in charge of Meggie unless she got better…until she got better.

That evening, they took their usual walk. Meggie scampered ahead, pausing often to examine a bug, a tiny flower or her footsteps in the dust.

Burke followed contentedly at a sedate pace, Jenny at his side. This was his favorite part of the day—sharing his love of the prairies with someone who seemed of like mind, enjoying his niece. More and more his love for her grew. He would do what he must in order to provide her with the best. Except send her away. They had only each other and he would not let her be taken elsewhere to be raised. Somehow they would manage. Surely Paquette would soon be back to her normal self.

He thought of those flashes in her eyes and wondered if Jenny had noticed anything. "Do you see any improvement in Paquette?"

She hesitated. "Sometimes I think she is getting better but then I think I've imagined it."

"I get the same feeling. I suppose that's a good sign."

She shrugged. "I have no idea."

"It's times like this I wonder where God is. Why He doesn't do something."

"You mean like make her better?"

"Of course." Why couldn't things be different out here? Not so challenging? Of course, it took the brave and strong to settle new lands. "Maybe I should sell the ranch. Go east. Move into a town. Not back to the cities but someplace civilized."

She spun around so fast that dust engulfed them. "Now why would you do that? I can't imagine you in a town, let alone a city." She glanced about. "I can't imagine you leaving all this. Why would you even consider it?"

"For Meggie." For Jenny. He couldn't ask her to live in the wilds. He snorted. Not that there was any point in asking her anything. She was set to marry the man her pa had chosen for her. Didn't matter where he lived, she wouldn't give him a second consideration. "Lena would want her raised to be a lady."

"So teach her how to be a lady at the same time as you teach her to live like a pioneer. The two aren't mutually exclusive."

He didn't answer. How could he? Yet he didn't want to live in town. Especially when it would make no difference to whether or not Jenny might consider him as a suitor.

"Besides, what would you do with Paquette? Leave her here to manage on her own?"

"I'd take her."

"Can you honestly see her in town? She'd go out of her mind."

"One night on the prairie seems to have done that to her already."

"So you're going to give up on her. Why not send

her to the asylum?" Her eyes flashed with anger and something harder, more challenging.

She was calling him a quitter. Blaming him for sending Flora away. "I didn't put Flora in the asylum. The authorities did. For her own protection. Her parents signed the papers."

She relented so fast the air rushed from her lungs. "I'm sorry. I had no right to say that. But it seems you expect all females to crack out here. It's a demeaning attitude, don't you think?"

He wanted to believe it could be otherwise. "If this land can destroy Paquette, do you think anyone can survive it?"

She crossed her arms and gave him a noble expression. "I certainly do. Women have pioneered alongside their men for centuries. Why is this situation any different?"

"It's the land." He waved to indicate the space around them. "It's lonely. Godforsaken, many say."

"And yet I feel like God is closer here than anywhere I've been. It's as if I have only to lift my hand heavenward to connect with Him."

Her voice sounded so content, so happy. Her eyes sparkled.

When she realized he watched her, she laughed. "Sorry. I didn't mean to sound so full of fancy."

"It isn't like you plan to stay."

She stared out at the prairie for a long time, silent

and still. He wondered if she even breathed. Then she jerked in air. "No, you're right. I am going back home as soon as Paquette is better."

"So this whole discussion is simply...what?" It didn't matter if she could survive the prairie or not. It didn't matter if he wanted her to stay or was convinced she must go. None of it mattered as much as the dust at his feet that would blow away overnight.

She flicked a glance at him. "I just don't want you making a mistake because you judge Meggie too weak to handle the challenges of this life."

"So you think leaving the ranch would be a mistake?"

"If you do it for the wrong reason."

He studied her. She kept her gaze on the horizon, though he knew from the way her lashes fluttered she was aware of his look. "Guess you'd know about doing things for the wrong reason."

That brought her full attention to him in a hurry. "Are you accusing me of having faulty motives?"

"Don't you? Aren't your reasons for letting your father choose your mate based on fear instead of trust? Wouldn't you consider that the wrong reason for doing anything?"

She tore her gaze from him, leaving him burning with regrets.

"I'm sorry. It's none of my business. Except—" He wouldn't say he cared. Because it was too weak a statement for the way he felt. Not that it mattered one hair. She meant to go home. And he would let her. Without a word of protest, knowing it was for her good.

"Come, Meggie. It's time to go back." She took the child by the hand and hurried them home, pausing only long enough for a curt good-night before she left him standing on the veranda.

Paquette had gone indoors, too. Burke had nothing to make him stay. Except his own wayward wishes.

Which he would deny with every breath he drew.

Jenny managed to ignore her thoughts as she prepared Meggie for bed and checked on Paquette. Then she couldn't avoid them. *So you think leaving the ranch would be a mistake?* He'd meant for him. But the words twisted through her like a scouring brush, erasing all her excuses and reasons for going home. Never before had a place made her feel so alive and—as she said to Burke—so close to God. To her shame, she'd never felt for any man the things she felt for Burke—as if their thoughts completed each other's, as if their hearts beat to the same rhythm.

Oh Father God, forgive me for such traitorous thoughts. You saved me from myself once before. Do so again, I beg. Don't let me ruin my life by following my heart. Please, God, help me. Strengthen me.

She prayed for a long time until finally her spirit was submissive.

Yet when she rose the next morning she felt relief, tinged with sorrow, that Paquette continued to be so confused. And she realized she hadn't even prayed for the woman's healing. *Oh God, forgive me. I don't even realize how selfish I am. Please help Paquette get better.*

Comforted by her faith, she hurried to make breakfast. She loved the challenge of coping with her limited supplies, the sheer bulk of food the men consumed and their enjoyment of everything she cooked. Thankfully she had observed Paquette at work and had insisted on helping despite the woman's initial protests, so she knew how to deal with the limitations.

She prepared the food and rang the bell. She wished she could avoid Burke but he crossed the yard with the others. Pushing her resolve into place, she vowed she would not meet his glance. But she couldn't resist and was disappointed when he had his face turned away from her. She stole looks several times during the meal. Each time he looked another direction. As if he didn't want to look at her. Couldn't bear to see her.

She couldn't blame him. He thought her weak because she intended to accept Ted's offer of marriage. Better safe than sorry. Only would she rather be safe? And where or what was safe? Pa seemed to think it lay in letting him guide her along paths of his choosing. Not that she for an instant thought he had anything but her best interests in mind.

Burke seemed to think safe meant living in a sheltered, settled, developed place and yet choosing a man on her own.

And her? What meant safety for her? Did she even know?

"I'll be sending someone to town for supplies after breakfast." Burke's reminder pulled her from trying to answer her own questions. "Anything you need?"

Happy for a chance to add a few things to the pantry, she said, "I'll make the list."

Burke nodded and left before she'd even started the list. Mac returned for it a few minutes later.

Of course, she wasn't disappointed Burke had sent someone else. Why should she be? They both knew this was temporary.

It was late afternoon before Mac returned. He brought in the supplies she ordered and two letters from home. She set them aside to read after she'd put the things away. But knowing they awaited her, she hurried through the task.

Meggie played contentedly at her feet, pushing her rag doll into a pot and covering it with a lid, then laughing when she pulled the lid away and the doll popped upright.

Jenny laughed at the little girl's play then turned her attention to the letters. She read the date on the postmarks and opened the earlier one first, reading notes from Ma, Pa and Sarah. Nothing but things she'd heard reiterated many times before she left. *Guard your tongue, but even more, guard your thoughts.* She'd tried. Perhaps not hard enough because she knew if Ma and Pa could read her thoughts, see how her heart responded when she was with Burke, they would be dismayed.

But she'd tried. Moreover, she intended to follow through on her promise to return and marry Ted. She'd adjust to her role in life.

Sighing, she opened the second letter. Her dismay grew with each line she read. It was as if Pa could see what she did even hundreds of miles away—proof he knew her better than she knew herself. A convincing reason to follow his guidance.

Daughter, he wrote. *Reading between the lines, I see evidence that your bold spirit has raised its head again. Your boldness is good but must be moderated with wisdom and submission. I don't mean submission to us, as your parents, but to God. You must use your God-given wisdom to discern wise choices from those that seem more alluring, more exciting. I think I need not tell you how important this is. Here is what I think you must do. You must make arrangements to return home posthaste. If you aren't satisfied Mr. Douglas's housekeeper can provide adequate care for Meggie at this time, consider alternatives. There are many, as I'm sure you're aware. Arranging for a nanny comes to my mind. But do whatever is necessary to complete your task. Do not let the temptation of new places divert you from what is best for you.*

He closed as her loving father.

His words blazed through her heart like a hot coal, burning away her pretense, exposing her foolish wishes…wants, really.

Pa was right. She had been using Paquette's illness as an excuse to stay when there were other avenues to explore.

She would write an advertisement for a nanny and send it for Pa to place in the paper back home. Why, there must be lots of young women seeking a way to head west. She thought of Burke and the possibilities with a young woman in residence. Well, perhaps there were some not-so-young ones looking for a chance to relocate, too.

There she went thinking only of herself again. Of course, the best thing for Meggie—and Burke—would be for him to marry. No reason her lungs should stiffen with protest.

She carefully considered the words then penned them on a separate sheet of paper before she wrote a reply to her parents.

If Dug meant to go to town again tomorrow, she would send the letter with him.

With no church in town, she had started having her own worship service. At first she had stayed in her bedroom and read the Bible and prayed while Meggie slept, but too soon she would be leaving this wonderful, free land. She would miss it. She couldn't think of a better place to worship God than outdoors. She didn't want to leave Meggie with Paquette so she took the child. "We're going for a walk," she told the older woman, though she wondered if Paquette, lost in her own world, would even notice her departure. Or wonder if they never returned.

Jenny walked a distance until she felt alone, away from observation from anyone back at the ranch, and rejoiced to see a few trees that promised a bit of shade. She made her way to them. "Meggie, you play here." She gathered some twigs that might interest the child then leaned against the trunk of a tree and opened her Bible. But she wasn't ready to read yet. Her thoughts twisted and turned.

It had been two weeks since she'd sent the letter to Ma and Pa. She hadn't told Burke her plans. Once she had some suitable applicants for him to consider, he would see the benefit of hiring a nanny. He would accept this was the best way. She couldn't stay, and

Meggie needed more care than anyone here could provide.

But try as she did, she couldn't prevent a blast of regret from sweeping through her. Someone else would take her place in caring for Meggie. And in caring for Burke.

Why must her heart be always so willful? Wanting things that were wrong, forbidden, dangerous?

Father God, forgive me for being so weak. Give me strength to face the future. To obey You through obeying my parents.

She clung to her faith, knowing God would strengthen and uphold her. Slowly, peace and resolve filled her soul. As Meggie sang a wordless tune, Jenny turned to her Bible. It opened to Isaiah chapter forty-three. She began to read. The words leapt from the page straight to her heart. "But now thus saith the Lord that created thee—"

Oh yes, God had made her. He understood her better than anyone.

She read on. "When thou passest through the waters, I will be with thee; and through the rivers, they shall not overflow thee; when thou walkest through the fire, thou shalt not be burned; neither shall the flame kindle upon thee."

Yes, Father God. I fear I am about to walk through the waters and the fire when I have to leave here.

Only by Your strength can I do what I know is right.

On and on she read, finding strength and comfort.

Burke watched Jenny and Meggie head out into the prairie. What were they doing? He thought of following them but for several days Jenny had gone out of her way to avoid him. He was at a loss to explain why. Apart from having told her she was returning to her parents and their plans for all the wrong reasons and accusing her of being afraid to act on her own behalf, he'd said and done nothing to make her pull back.

He chuckled. That was more than enough, especially for Jenny. She didn't take kindly to being called a coward in any terms.

She'd proven herself capable of running his house as Paquette continued to wander in her mind. Occasionally he caught a flash of his housekeeper's old self—sharp eyes, quick wit—but it seemed to fade as soon as it came. Lucky reported seeing her leave the ranch a few times. Burke wondered if Lucky imagined it. He'd never seen Paquette leave the veranda.

He bent over the harness he cleaned. A nice Sunday afternoon task. Until Jenny came, the ranch had paid little attention to the Sabbath. Perhaps worked a little slower as Dug and Mac rose late and bleary-eyed.

Things had shifted over the past weeks. Burke

couldn't say how or when. Only that it had something to do with Jenny. And perhaps a tiny bit to do with his prayer for help to find Paquette. Seemed to be no way he could deny God guided him that night. And if that were so, did God care about all the details of his life? He couldn't quite get his head around the idea yet but, bit by bit, he had begun to allow God into his life.

He prayed more often. Especially for Paquette's healing. For wisdom in being Meggie's guardian. And for Jenny? Every time he tried to pray for her, he came smack hard against raging conflict. He wanted her to stay. Knew she couldn't. Wouldn't. She was set on returning to this Ted fellow. But even more than that, he wouldn't ask her. If this country could destroy Paquette, what would it eventually do to Jenny? His thoughts circled endlessly on that dreadful question. He must deny his feelings for her. For her sake. Even if she were to give him any encouragement, any indication she might have changed her mind about Ted. Which she never had.

Head down, he rubbed at the leather with the saddle soap. Tried to keep his mind focused on the task. But his thoughts insisted on racing after Jenny. She'd been gone a long time. Had she gotten turned around? Lost? If it could happen to Paquette—

Shoot. He wouldn't be able to breathe easy until he was certain of her safety.

"Hey, Lucky," he called to the man lounging in the open door of the barn. "I'm going for a walk."

Lucky chuckled. "Saw Miss Jenny headed out. Wondered how long it would take for you to go after her."

"I'm not—I didn't plan—" He waved one arm dismissively. "Just want to make sure she's safe."

"Yeah, boss. You go do that."

Lucky's chortling humor followed him down the path. He walked to the end of the trail and looked around. Saw no sign of them. Glanced at the ground. Little footprints led to the right. He jogged that direction. Climbed a slight rise. In the distance he saw a bit of white. Meggie at play close to some trees. He strained, glimpsed Jenny against one tree, sitting still. Was she hurt?

He shuddered, remembering how Flora had run into the prairie. His memory echoed with her mad screams, sending prickles up and down his spine.

It took every ounce of his will to drive the picture away. But he couldn't edge away the alarm and broke into a full-out run, crossing the prairie in great strides, gulping in dusty air.

Jenny turned at his approach. Sprang to her feet at his urgent haste.

"What's wrong? Is it Paquette?"

He reached her side, gasping air for his starved lungs. "Are you…okay?"

She knotted her eyebrows. "I'm fine. Why?"

He leaned over his knees, sucking hard to ease his breathing. As soon as he could talk without panting, he faced her. "What are you doing out here? Have you any idea how easy it is to get lost? And to bring Meggie with you? That's the height of stupidity." His anger drove from his mouth words he knew were wrong, offensive.

Her eyes narrowed. Her mouth pursed. She tucked in her chin and looked ready to fight. Then she blinked and her expression shifted. A warm acknowledging of something sweet and precious filled her eyes.

She'd read his worry. Perhaps guessed it went further than simple concern for her safety, or Meggie's. He sucked back his feelings, pulling his impossible love behind a fortress. But she had managed to breech the walls, break down the thick logs erected to protect his heart. He should consider her intrusion a defeat. He could not. No more than he could welcome it. Nothing had changed. It could not be.

She again read his shift of thought and her eyes grew wary. "I'm not exactly a fool. I take note of my surroundings. The ranch is right over there. In fact, you can see our footsteps in the grass."

He didn't need to look to see the evidence in the way the grass bent at each step.

"And over there is a big grove of trees. You can't see them but I see the birds rising from the branches.

And Buffalo Hollow is that way. If I look really hard I can see the top of the water tower."

He forced his gaze away from her lest she read his surprise. How many noticed such tiny details? Only those born on the prairie or having spent many seasons learning such things. Amazing she should be so quick to take note.

But why torment himself with such things? Nothing had changed. She was going back east because no matter now astute she was about her bearings, the prairies could destroy anyone. The words echoed through his insides like the wail of a prairie storm.

He would not meet her eyes again. Instead, he sat by Meggie. "Hello, Meg peg. Whatcha doing?"

She waved a handful of twigs and chattered non-stop for two full minutes.

He chuckled softly. "I didn't understand one word."

She nodded, seemingly content with his response.

He picked her up, tossing her in the air until she giggled. Then sat and plunked her in his lap facing him.

Her eyes sparkled with mischief. "Ticco ticco." She dug her little fingers into his ribs and giggled.

"You little tease." He wrapped his arms around her and shook her until she squealed with laughter. They tumbled to the ground and rolled around tickling and laughing.

Finally spent, he sat up and pulled Meggie to his lap, holding her with her back pressed to his chest. Not ready to quit, she squirmed, trying to dig into his ribs again. When she realized he wasn't going to let her, she settled on his knees, resting her head beneath his chin.

He loved her, could pour all his love into her life. No need for anyone else to share with.

Sadness, reluctance and resignation weaved in and out of his thoughts, pulling them together so he couldn't separate one from the other.

"Are you ready to go home?" He spoke to the air in front of him, not wanting to directly address Jenny. Besides, he reminded himself sharply, the ranch wasn't her home.

"We're ready."

At least she didn't correct him.

They returned to the ranch. He left them at the veranda and escaped to the corrals where he could be alone with his useless wishes and regrets.

Chapter Eleven

Over the next few days, Burke found plenty of excuses to be away from the ranch. He rode the entire countryside, checking on his cows and the few neighbors they had. He filled his saddlebags to stay away for several days. At least that was his plan. Seems he couldn't keep away more than one night. Told himself he needed to check on Paquette, spend time with Meggie. He'd taken to putting her to bed when he was around. He enjoyed it immensely, recalling lullabies and nursery rhymes from his childhood.

But as he returned to the ranch, it was neither Meggie nor Paquette's face he ached to see before his lungs remembered their job was to fill with air.

It wasn't until Jenny glanced up, a quick flash of awareness—that she just as quickly masked—lighting her eyes, did he feel he had come home.

How would he survive when she left? And leave

she must. Just as soon as Paquette was better. He denied he felt relief that the poor housekeeper showed very little improvement.

His plan had been to spend tonight camping out far from the ranch, but here he was riding back, anticipating the supper Jenny had prepared, Jenny sitting at his left as he ate—

Enough. He couldn't force himself to stay away, but he could refuse to let thoughts of her color every moment.

As he neared home, a buggy approached the ranch. Who could possibly be visiting? He reined in at the end of the corrals to watch.

The buggy drove up to the house, and Mr. Zach jumped down to assist someone descending—a woman in a gray traveling dress, her hair hidden by a bonnet. She paused at the steps and waited for Zach to lift down two cases. Two cases? Who was this woman? And why was she planning to park here long enough to require two cases?

He urged his mount into action and rode toward the house. Lucky stood gaping at the corral as Burke dropped to the ground. "Take my horse."

"Yes, boss. Company?"

"'Pears so."

"You invite someone?"

"Nope." And seeing he was boss, no one else had the right.

The woman disappeared into the kitchen, Zach at her heels with the two bags.

Burke's jaw muscles clenched as he watched those two bags disappear inside.

"Best go see who it is," Lucky said, sounding as if it surely meant bad news.

Burke supposed he was thinking how it had been when Flora descended on them with her whining and complaining, her snobbish ways. Jenny had been a breath of blessed relief after that disastrous visit.

He didn't expect this unannounced, uninvited visitor to be from the same refreshing breeze.

"We'll soon see what this is all about." He strode across the yard, ignoring the steps as he jumped to the veranda and thudded around to the kitchen.

Over the shoulder of the visitor, Jenny's gaze jerked to him. Her face flooded with guilt. Whoever this was, Jenny had something to do with her presence. And he wanted an explanation.

"Burke, I'd like to introduce Miss Smythe."

The woman turned. "Pleased to meet you, sir." She lowered her eyes and gave a little curtsy, then gave him a look that made his mouth want to pucker.

He could hardly guess the woman's age. Her face was young, her eyes and mouth old, as if life had worn her out. The skin around her eyes seemed too tight. Likely because her hair had been pulled back so severely.

"That's Smythe with a y. I'm pleased to meet my charge's guardian."

Paquette sat at the table. She started to mumble rapidly at the woman's brash announcement.

He didn't spare Paquette a glance. "Your charge?" He would not sputter. He shifted to study Jenny. "You know anything about this?"

"I do. Yes."

Miss Smythe with a y cleared her throat. "I was given to understand—"

He grabbed Jenny's elbow and dragged her toward the door. "I think you better explain. In private."

"Sir, if I may inquire—" He left poor Miss Smythe protesting to the door as it slapped shut behind Jenny. He knew a nasty sense of satisfaction when she yelped and jumped to avoid getting slammed in the back.

He didn't release her until they were ten feet from the veranda, then he faced her squarely. "Explain."

"I didn't expect someone to just turn up."

"That doesn't explain anything. Who is this woman and what is she doing here? With two large bags."

"Her name is Miss Smythe. With a *y*." Jenny flashed him a glance full of caution and pleading.

He wasn't about to let her off and made a warning noise. "Don't repeat what I already know. Why is she here?"

Jenny sighed. "It was Pa's idea." She paused as if hoping that would be explanation enough.

He crossed his arms, signifying he wasn't satisfied.

She waggled her hands. "I don't know where to start."

"Why is she here?"

"Pa thought I was taking too long to return so he suggested I arrange for a nanny. So I asked him to put an ad—"

"You what?"

"I arranged—" She said it so meekly he hardly recognized her voice.

"That's what I thought you said. A nanny. What do I want with a nanny?"

Her look scorched him. "I don't know what *you* want with one, but Meggie needs someone to care for her."

Shock at her presumption gave way to a long deep ache reaching to the horizon and back. He'd been lulled into thinking she would stay until Paquette was better. Even thought she enjoyed the time at the ranch, but seems she couldn't wait to get away. "So you did this behind my back?"

"Burke." Her voice sounded strained, as if it hurt to admit her underhanded, sneaky behavior.

As well it should.

"I didn't expect someone to just show up. I thought

I'd get some letters and I'd show them to you and discuss it."

"You had it all figured out."

"Except Pa chose the one he thought most suitable and sent her." She waved a letter to indicate her father's communication on the matter.

Most suitable? Likely the only one Jenny's father could persuade to come out here. "How long do you figure she'll stay? One night of coyotes howling, one wind storm screaming around the house and—"

"I described the situation and the setting. I'm certain Pa would have checked the woman out."

"I don't want another woman here." The words came out sharp and bitter. "I suppose you picked someone you thought would be a suitable wife for me."

"Pa picked her out. Not me."

They stared hard at each other, her look pleading and regretful, his likely as accusing and angry as he felt. His heart seemed to have developed a pocket for carrying a ten-pound weight. It lay low in his chest—heavy and unresponsive. She obviously couldn't wait to leave.

He had to drag a reminder from some dark distant corner of his mind that he wanted her to go. Would insist on it, in fact. This country was not for women.

"She won't stay."

"If she'd only stay long enough for Paquette to get better and until Meggie is a little older and doesn't need so much supervision." Her voice echoed his doubt that either of those things would happen.

"You've overstepped your rights in doing this, but perhaps it's for the best. You need to get back to your Pa's plans for your life." He failed to keep the unreasonable bitterness from his words. He didn't want Jenny to stay. Perhaps if he kept saying it he would eventually believe it.

He had nothing more to give. It would likely take the rest of his life for his heart to relearn how to beat solidly.

Jenny forced herself to smile as she explained again how to wash Meggie's clothes.

Miss Smythe—who said she preferred to be called such and refused to reveal her Christian name—scowled deeply. Jenny was convinced the woman had long ago lost the use of the muscles allowing her to smile.

She made herself stop. Knew her criticism was unfair. It was only because she envied the woman this opportunity.

If only she could stay.

Stop. Stop wishing for things that don't belong to you. She couldn't stay. So why did it hurt to see someone who made it possible for her to leave?

Because she was—as always—given to wild, rash actions. Only this time she would not allow herself to follow her wayward heart.

Miss Smythe proved to be kind and gentle with Meggie. To her credit, after some initial shock, she had agreed to help with meal preparation until Paquette could manage on her own.

Paquette glowered constantly at this intruder—the only word she used in addressing Miss Smythe.

"She's not been well," Jenny explained. "Once she's feeling better…" Paquette had improved enough that she often insisted on doing some of the cooking. But she spent the rest of her time in some kind of vague fog.

Miss Smythe had been on the ranch four days. Four tense days as Burke alternated between sitting at the table, glumly watching Miss Smythe try to learn the intricacies of the primitive aspects of the ranch, or gulping his meals, giving Jenny a dark look then rushing out the door like he couldn't bear to be in the same room.

Meggie had just wakened from her nap and played cheerfully with Miss Smythe. "Mith," her name for the woman, "see beads." She silently appealed to Paquette to be allowed to share her beads.

Paquette shook her head. "No beads. Mine."

"Look at your dolly." Miss Smythe wisely diverted

Meggie's attention by making the rag doll dance and sing.

It was a good time to leave them alone to see how Miss Smythe managed. And Jenny longed to wander the prairie and pack as many memories as possible into her soul. "Do you mind if I go for a walk?"

Miss Smythe looked up and grimaced. "You're going out in this wind?"

Jenny laughed. "I like it." They'd had this conversation before. Miss Smythe refused to venture outside when the wind blew. Jenny warned her it meant she'd spend most of her days indoors.

Miss Smythe shuddered. "I don't mind."

Jenny refrained from asking how it would affect Meggie. The child loved being outside. Burke would have to sort out the situation without her interference.

"I'll be back in an hour or so." The wind hit her a few feet from the shelter of the house. It pushed her skirts around her legs, tugged her hair from the pins that bound it. She laughed and let it carry her along until she was a mile from the ranch. There she stood, her face to the sky, her eyes closed, and let the wind rage around her and sweep through her.

Father God, cleanse me from my wayward, sinful thoughts. Help me keep my eyes set on the path before me. Help me graciously accept the loving guidance of my parents.

She stood that way a long time seeking peace and strength. Then, her resolve firmly in place, she drank in the scenery around her, trying to memorize each detail—the way the horizon turned gray and misty, rising and falling ever so subtly, the endless sky that at first glance appeared all one color, but with closer study shifted through a range of blues. She found a grassy spot and sat down, breathing deeply of the scents—sage, something sweet and spicy—the source of which she'd never been able to locate—and teases of scented flowers. She sneezed at the pungent aroma of nearby yarrow. The minute details of the place fascinated her. Each blade of grass so unique. Tiny flowers hiding amongst the grass. God surely had created a marvelous world. Never had she been so aware of His hand.

If God so clothe the grass of the field...

He would surely give her all she needed, too. Satisfaction with her life, peace with her surroundings.

I am ready to do Your will, O my God.

She remained there a long time, soaking her senses in the beauty and allure of the prairie and finding rest in obedience to a God she loved and trusted.

Finally, reluctantly, she pushed to her feet. It was time to return. If Miss Smythe were agreeable, Jenny would leave by the end of the week. She could not deny a great ache at the thought, but she was at peace with what she must do.

The wind buffeted her on her way, forcing her to lean into the blast. She laughed and a gust stole her breath and carried the laugh across the prairie.

Oh how she would miss this bold, powerful land.

I am ready to do Your will, O God.

She reached the yard and paused at the wail the wind carried. A different sound than the usual one it made around the house. She pushed on. Suddenly she recognized the sound—Meggie screaming in terror. Jenny picked up her skirts and ran into the wind. A few feet from the house she heard another voice—Miss Smythe's, pleading and panicked.

Jenny fought her way against the wind until—gasping—she reached the shelter of the veranda. She flung open the door and took in the scene.

Meggie sat on the floor, surrounded by Paquette's beads, shuddering with her screams.

Across the room, Paquette held a mop aloft, threatening Miss Smythe who had backed into the corner, her arms over her head.

Jenny kicked the beads away from Meggie to keep her from putting one in her mouth. "Shh, Meggie, sweetie. You're fine." She'd tend the baby as soon as she dealt with Paquette.

She approached the older woman. "Paquette, what are you doing?"

Paquette made a low guttural sound, like a wild animal growling.

"You don't want to hurt anyone." She calmly plucked the mop from Paquette's hands and dropped it to the floor, then pulled the woman into her arms. "Oh, Paquette, what's wrong with you? What's going on in that head of yours?" She rocked until Paquette sighed and relaxed.

"Boss," Lucky called into the barn. Burke was repairing a hole in the wall where Ebony had kicked in protest when Burke tried to saddle him. Crazy horse. Yet he'd seen Jenny stroking the horse and talking to it more than once when she was unaware of him watching. "Awful racket from the house."

"Yeah?"

"Think you might like to check."

Burke knew that tone of voice. Lucky meant Burke should check *now* so he put down his tools and headed out. As soon as he stepped from the barn, he heard the noise and knew why Lucky was concerned. "It's Meggie." She screamed with terror. He vaulted the fence and galloped for the house, the skin over his spine crawling at the way she cried. If someone had hurt that little girl—

He thudded across the veranda and through the open door. Meggie sat on the floor, crying her heart out. Jenny wrapped Paquette in her arms, murmuring calmly. Miss Smythe huddled in a corner. She couldn't seem to take her eyes from a mop on the floor in front of her. He took it all in with a glance. What was going on? Had Paquette attacked the woman? Had she totally lost her mind? It happened too often. Sorrow laced with acceptance tore through his insides like a flood tearing up roots of hope and flickers of dreams, dragging them away in a rush of dirty raging water.

Yes, he'd allowed himself to hope—he couldn't even say what he'd hoped for. But seeing Paquette like this made it impossible to hope—or dream—or even wish.

This country was no place for Jenny.

He scooped Meggie from the floor and wrapped her to his chest. She sobbed against his shoulder, clinging to him fiercely. He would protect this sweet child from any danger.

Would she be able to survive this harsh land?

He would teach her how. She'd grow with it.

Like Paquette had?

If he had to, he would send Meggie away. If that's what it took to keep her whole and well. A silent groan gripped his throat. His knees melted beneath him and he sank to the bench.

Jenny turned as if checking on Meggie. She noticed him, her eyes widening as they met his.

In that moment of truth something shifted inside

him. His fear collided with his dreams and exploded into a thousand flashing fragments nipping at his thoughts. It took several seconds to gather up all the pieces and stuff them back behind the log wall he'd so carefully constructed. "What's going on here?"

Miss Smythe shook her skirts and smoothed her hair. "That woman is out of her mind. She should be locked up."

His gut tightened. His thoughts skittered a protest. Not in the asylum. Not like Flora. Paquette would wither and die in such a place.

Paquette pulled from Jenny's arms and sank to a chair. "Not crazy. My beads. Not touch 'em, her."

"She attacked me. She's dangerous."

Burke had seen it before, how the land, the loneliness, the sound of the wind drove normally calm people into demented rages. Sometimes locking them up was the only way to keep them and others safe— but must everyone in his life end up there?

"Paquette would never hurt anyone. She was only warning you not to touch her beads. They're her most prized possession. We all understand that."

Miss Smythe sniffed loudly and disdainfully. "She's out of her mind. No normal person acts like that."

Paquette peered up at Miss Smythe. "Paquette not crazy." She jabbed a finger at Miss Smythe. "You not stay 'ere. Not belong, you." She turned to Jenny and jabbed her bony finger at her. "You stay. Not her."

Miss Smythe nodded. "I agree. I absolutely will not stay here. It's not safe. The rest of you will be murdered in your beds." She steamed down the hall to the bedroom.

Jenny's eyes were pleading when she looked at Burke. "She isn't crazy. I know it. She wouldn't hurt anyone. You must not send her away."

Burke understood she meant Paquette. "I don't want to but—" He couldn't put Jenny and Meggie at risk.

Another problem bucked into his mind. "Miss Smythe is leaving. Paquette's…ill. Who will care for Meggie?"

"I can stay until you make other arrangements."

"I can't expect you to do that." Any more than he could continually fight the way his wants warred against the knowledge Jenny must leave. Not only was she set on going, he was now even more set on seeing her leave before she suffered the same fate as Paquette and Flora and so many others.

Yes, it seems some women could survive the prairies. But they were few and far between. And he would not stand by and wait to see who would be next to find the country intolerable.

He stared at Paquette, still unable to believe one

bred and born on the prairie had fallen victim to its subtle dangers.

She met his gaze unblinkingly. She was trying to tell him something. But what? Slowly it became clear she showed no sign of confusion, no terror, no anger. Only certainty, as if he would understand her silent message.

He shook his head. "Paquette—?"

She ducked away.

Miss Smythe returned, dragging her bag and looking a bit ruffled, as if she'd hurried to pack everything. "I insist on a ride to town immediately. I can't abide this endless wind."

Burke's gaze rested on Paquette's head. There was more going on here than he understood. "I'll get Lucky to take you." He wouldn't leave Meggie and Jenny with Paquette until he figured out what it was.

Lucky bemoaned having to interrupt his work to make this trip. "Not that I'm sorry to see her go. She ain't our kind of lady. Not like Jenny."

Burke sighed. "Jenny ain't staying."

"You tried asking her?"

"She's got a fellow back home."

"Huh. Don't see no wedding ring. Seems to me that leaves lots of possibilities."

"It's not that simple."

"Boss, nothing is, but did that keep you from

starting a ranch in the middle of nothing but grass and sky?"

"That's different."

"How?"

"Cause grass and sky didn't have anything to say about me being here."

Lucky snorted a laugh. "Seems they have something to say every minute of the day. Some people listen—like Flora. Others—like you and Miss Jenny—just sing along."

He stared at the man. "I perceive you're a dreamer."

Lucky shifted and refused to meet Burke's gaze. "Nope. Just saying it the way I see it. And the way I see it is you're running from the chance every woman might be like Flora. Running from what's right in front of your nose. Boss, maybe it's time you stopped running."

"It's you who don't see what's right in front of all of us."

"Yeah?"

"Jenny intends to go back east. I intend to let her. Just as soon as Paquette is well enough to watch Meggie."

"Yeah, boss." Lucky hitched up the wagon and drove to the house.

A few minutes later, Miss Smythe departed, sitting regally at Lucky's side.

Burke stared after them a long time. He had no

regrets at seeing the back of Miss Smythe with a y, but the reprieve provided only more torment. Because nothing had changed.

Jenny intended to leave.

He intended to see she did.

Jenny knew it was wrong. This gladness that she must stay a bit longer. Ma and Pa would surely warn her to put an end to her foolish behavior. But they weren't here. And she could hardly leave Meggie with only some busy men and Paquette to watch her. Even Pa would understand that argument.

Burke still stood on the veranda watching Miss Smythe disappear down the trail. What was he thinking? Likely that he might never get rid of Jenny.

How ironic that Miss Smythe, who had nothing to return to, couldn't wait to leave while Jenny, who had iron-solid reasons to return, found her heart shriveling like a drought-stricken plant at the knowledge she couldn't stay. Not only did she love the land but— forbidden as it was—she had grown exceptionally fond of the ranch owner.

Burke turned suddenly, catching her staring at him, her heart in her eyes. A gamut of emotions crossed his eyes—sadness perhaps at losing the nanny, though he hadn't ever shown anything but long-suffering tolerance for her so perhaps it was sadness over Paquette's behavior. Then his eyes widened as he took in her naked caring and regret. At that moment, they were more honest with each other than at any time since she'd landed on his doorstep. Silently they acknowledged a common want—she wanted to stay, he wanted her to.

Guilt burned up her neck and pooled in her eyes, causing them to sting. She ducked away. Would she never learn to temper her desires with reason and submission?

Burke's breath huffed out.

She understood her inappropriateness left him surprised and likely a little puzzled. After all, she'd made it plain from the beginning she wouldn't stay.

Paquette pushed past her. "Make supper, me."

Her words effectively ended Jenny's mental wrangling. She blinked at Paquette. The woman sounded strong and focused. Not at all like she'd been since her night on the prairie. "Paquette?"

"I fine, me." She pulled out pots and handed a pan to Jenny. "Get potatoes, you."

Jenny shot a questioning look at Burke. Was she imagining this sudden change in Paquette? She knew from the way Burke looked at the older woman he was as startled by her behavior as she.

Slowly he met her eyes and gave a slight lift of his shoulders. For a moment they considered each other, silently assessing this new development.

Paquette saw Jenny with the still empty basin and grunted. "Need potatoes."

Jenny hurried to get them from the bin.

Burke shifted Meggie to his other arm as he crossed the room to face Paquette. "Are you all right?"

Paquette giggled. "I fine."

"Did something happen out on the prairie? Were you hurt?"

She giggled again. "Not hurt."

Jenny stared at the woman, a suspicion creeping through her mind. "Paquette, were you pretending?"

Another giggle before Paquette turned to rearrange the pots as if they required all her attention.

"Why would you do that?"

Paquette turned, her black eyes flashing. "Show everybody you need to stay. You belong here, you."

Jenny gasped. Heat stung her cheeks. No doubt Paquette had seen the way Jenny watched Burke and read—misread—what it meant. It meant nothing but normal curiosity and interest. Oh, if only she believed it. But she could ignore it…or try. "Paquette, I can't stay. You know that." She told the woman about Ted.

Paquette snorted. "Die like grass in winter back there."

Jenny couldn't face either of them, certain her

longing and pain would reveal itself so she gave her complete and undivided attention to preparing the potatoes. "I'll be just fine."

She told herself the same thing about a thousand times an hour over the next few days. She'd notified Pa Miss Smythe had left. Knew he'd interview other young ladies for the post. But until then she could stay.

Once she got back home, she assured herself constantly, she would remember all the lessons Ma had taught her on proper behavior. She'd remember and she'd apply them and God would surely give her the peace she longed for.

In the meantime, she intended to enjoy her reprieve and hoard up memories to last a lifetime so she took long walks, sometimes alone, often with Meggie and rarely with Burke. She missed his company, sensed he pulled back as if he couldn't wait for her to leave.

She returned to the ranch after a pleasant hour of wandering around, expecting to be there when Meggie wakened. A tail of dust barreled down the trail toward the ranch.

No doubt the new nanny.

She pulled to a halt beside the corrals.

Burke sauntered over and leaned on the top rail. "Let's hope she's better than Miss Smythe. Preferably someone a little more seasoned. Tough yet kind."

A little thrill bubbled through her at his desire

for an older woman. "You should be looking for a wife."

"I don't need a wife. Don't want one." His vehemence tore a bloody strip from her heart and left her gasping. He couldn't be much clearer than that.

There would never be a place for Jenny out here. He only wanted someone to get Meggie big enough to ride with him.

The buggy pulled to the house. The dust wrapped around it, momentarily obscuring it from view. Then the tail of dust drifted on and revealed a man and woman. She didn't recognize the woman whom she assumed would be the new nanny, but the man was familiar.

Jenny blinked. "Pa?"

Chapter Twelve

Her pa? He'd come? Burke immediately straightened and stepped back from the fence, wondering if the man had seen how he leaned close to Jenny, wanting to breathe the scent of wild grasses and prairie wind she carried with her like she'd found a way to bottle them into a perfume. "What's he doing here?"

"I can't imagine. He must have left Ted in charge of the store."

Ah, the elusive Ted. Perhaps he'd asked Mr. Archibald to check on Jenny. Only one way to find out. "You going to introduce us?" He headed toward the pair as Mr. Zach lifted down bags. More bags. He hated seeing them land on the veranda. It meant more upset, and even worse, facing the inevitable—a nanny so Jenny could leave.

It's what he wanted. So he told himself time after time but Lucky's words had built a sturdy home in his heart and would not be ignored. "She sings with the prairie."

As if she was part of it. So long as a person didn't fight the land, they might survive.

Not that any of this made a difference. They'd both chosen a path diverging from this point.

Jenny fell in at his side.

Her father saw them and jogged over to hug Jenny. "Daughter, you are looking well." He examined her closely, no doubt to assure himself she was well in every way.

She hugged him back then turned to Burke. "Pa, this is Meggie's guardian, Burke Edwards."

Mr. Archibald shook his hand and gave him a hard, direct look.

Burke met the man's gaze without flinching. He had nothing to hide, nothing to be ashamed of. But he guarded his heart lest the man guess at his true feelings for his daughter. "Welcome. Come in."

Mr. Archibald waved toward the waiting woman. "Miss Morgan has agreed to come as your nanny. With your approval, of course."

Burke instantly didn't approve. The woman was older, which was good, but she looked as if life carried a dreadful odor. He couldn't imagine letting someone with such a sour expression care for Meggie. How soon before his little niece developed the same attitude? "Let's go inside and talk." He held the door and ushered them in.

Paquette sat on her chair, her arms across her chest, glowering at them. She'd been most cheerful these past few days despite Jenny's insistence she could not stay as Paquette wanted.

"Could we have tea?" he asked Paquette.

She only scowled deeper.

"I'll make it," Jenny said.

He wanted to refuse but Paquette in such a mood would not be reasoned with. He asked about the trip and listened to the comments while a whirlwind of protests filled his mind. He didn't want another nanny.

"Mr. Edwards—" Jenny's father addressed him.

"Please, call me Burke."

"I hope you find Miss Morgan satisfactory because I have come to take my daughter home."

Pain ripped through him. He pushed it away and nodded, his tongue as useless as a hunk of wood. Was this not what he wanted? Had wanted from the first time he set eyes on her? For her to go back to the safety and security of the east?

No. His heart cried. No. No. A thousand times no.

He could not look at Jenny. Could not let her see how he felt.

"I'm sure if you've checked her out, she'll be more

than satisfactory." He directed his words to Jenny's father.

Paquette began to mumble and sway.

The tension in the room grew. Burke suspected it was exactly what Paquette hoped would happen. Despite his resolve, he glanced at Jenny. His heart lurched at the hunger he saw. Then she glanced at Paquette, and when her gaze returned to him he saw only concern for Paquette and knew he'd been mistaken in thinking there had been anything more.

The kettle whistled, and she hurried to the stove to pour the water. She cut each of them a piece of cake she'd made earlier and served it on individual plates then poured tea, all the while ignoring Paquette's dark looks.

Meg fussed in the other room.

"I'll get her."

Burke could practically feel her relief as she slipped away, leaving him to listen to a litany of Miss Morgan's qualifications. He could certainly find no fault with her experience. But she lacked the joy of life Jenny revealed.

How would he ever get used to its absence?

Jenny scooped Meggie into her arms and held her close. Meggie, only half awake, didn't mind and snuffled against her chest.

"Oh, Meggie, what am I going to do? I don't want

to leave you with a stranger." She shuddered back a sob. "I don't want to leave you at all." Any more than she wanted to leave this place. Or the man who owned it. She wanted to be part of this great adventure of building a home and a future in this raw, new land.

Meggie squirmed.

"You're ready to be up, aren't you? Well, let's go. We have company." She returned to the kitchen. Meggie saw the strangers and ducked her head against Jenny's shoulder. "This shy young lady is Meggie. Meggie, can you say hello to Miss Morgan and my father?"

Meggie turned her head enough to peak out at them. "'Lo." She saw Burke and reached for him. She sat proudly on his lap and stole glances at the two strangers. She'd met Pa a few times but had obviously forgotten him.

Jenny hovered in the background, not wanting to sit at the table. Somehow sharing tea with Pa and the new nanny made the woman's presence far too real.

And the reality of Jenny's situation far too final.

Pa agreed Meggie should have a few days to get used to Miss Morgan. Some very uncharitable corner of Jenny's mind hoped there would be a serious flaw in Miss Morgan's character or references or even her presence, like perhaps a bad smell or an impossible accent that would make it unsuitable for her to stay. She laughed at an accent being a problem, seeing as Paquette's speech was often a challenge to understand, especially when she was riled about something and since Miss Morgan's arrival, she'd been plenty riled. Jenny acknowledged another uncharitable thought. It felt good to have Paquette defensive on her behalf.

But Miss Morgan was the epitome of an ideal nanny. She established a routine, spent time playing games with Meggie and taught her better table manners than most of the others at the ranch exhibited. Jenny hid her amusement at the way the men sat up straighter and used their utensils better when Miss Morgan joined them. Often she chose to feed Meggie before the men came in because it better suited her schedule. Once Paquette realized this, she made certain most of the meals were delayed until after Meggie and Miss Morgan had eaten.

But it must end soon. Pa could not be away long. Jenny had shown him some of her favorite places. He spent much time with Burke and the other men, had even gone away on a three-day trip to check on the cattle.

But she still had things she longed to show him. "Pa, would you like to go for a walk?"

"Love to, daughter." He'd been working on an

unfinished window frame. "Trying to make myself useful while I'm here." He put his tools aside.

She glanced around. No longer did she notice all the things that needed completing—the rails on the veranda that Miss Morgan had commented on: "T'would be much safer for Meggie if they were put up." But seeing the place through Pa's eyes, she grew aware of its defects. "Burke lost interest when his marriage fell through."

She'd told Pa in a letter about poor Flora.

"Where to this sunny afternoon?" He pulled his hat down more firmly against the wind.

"Let's just walk." She'd caught up on family news and events around Center City. She'd heard all about Ted's wonderful forward-thinking suggestions for the store. Today she just wanted to enjoy the prairie. They walked two or three miles from the ranch. "This is such beautiful country, don't you think?"

He smiled his gentle smile. "Seems a lonely place."

"Pa, it's teeming with life. Look." She knelt to part a few blades of grass and revealed tiny white phlox. "You just have to learn to look."

Pa squatted beside her. "I guess you've learned where to look."

She heard something in his voice, perhaps a suggestion of admiration, and turned to study his face.

But he lifted his face to glance toward the horizon. "It's a big land."

The wind caught his hat and tossed it to the ground, bowling it along. Jenny laughed and chased after it. She caught it and handed it back.

"Windy, too," Pa said.

"I know. Doesn't it make you want to become a kite and sail in the wind?"

Pa chuckled and pulled her against his side. "I have to admit it doesn't."

She turned away to pretend interest in something in the distance. Of course Pa didn't understand. He would think her enthusiasm for a place she must leave behind inappropriate. Another sign of her wayward wildness.

"Come, I have something else to show you." She led him toward the corrals.

"Is it a surprise or can you tell me where you're taking me?"

"I want to show you my special friend."

"Oh."

She knew without looking his eyebrows would have almost disappeared under his hat and she laughed. "It's a horse. See." She pointed toward Ebony's pen. "You stay here until I make sure he'll let you close. Everyone else thinks he's wild."

"Jenny, are you being foolhardy here?"

"No, Pa. I'm not. Ebony is my friend." She

stepped closer, murmuring to the horse who eyed Pa a moment, then decided he was harmless and trotted over to greet Jenny. She stroked his muzzle and scratched his ears. "I'm going to miss you, big guy. I hoped I'd be here long enough to persuade you to let the men ride you."

Ebony snorted and Jenny realized Pa had moved closer.

"He's a beauty, for sure. Is he broke?"

"Not yet. He won't let anyone but me get close to him. Though he isn't too nervous with you this close." But as she spoke, Ebony snorted and raced away, bucking and acting like he meant to destroy every man-made object he could reach.

"I'm surprised Burke let you near him. He's wild."

She reluctantly turned from the horse to face Pa. "He didn't know I was coming out here until it was too late to say anything."

"Jenny, you're bound to get yourself into trouble with your disregard for caution."

"Pa, I know. I try and guard my thoughts and actions. But Ebony was an honest mistake. I had no idea he was so wild. He isn't around me."

"Sometimes horses have been mistreated by men and will let a woman handle them."

"I suppose that might be the reason." So many

questions and doubts filled her mind. "Pa, why do I find submission so difficult? Sometimes I think God must have made a mistake when He created me. I should have been born a man so I could do something like build a ranch in this new land or..." She couldn't finish. Didn't even know what she wanted to say. Except the life she would return to seemed constricting. Rules were fine. She knew they served a good purpose. But she craved so much more than being a proper lady. She'd found it here on the ranch, in the midst of the raw prairie, but it would be denied her.

Pa gripped her shoulder. "Daughter, God makes no mistakes. He certainly didn't make one when He created you. 'You are fearfully and wonderfully made,' as it says in Psalm one hundred and thirty-nine, verse fourteen."

She waggled her head. She couldn't argue with what God's word said, yet so often it felt like she didn't belong in her life.

"Jenny, you must learn to accept God's will in your life. Once you do, you will find peace and contentment."

"I know." She would obey her parents, and thus obey God, only she didn't find peace and contentment, she just found emptiness. "I know." Peace would surely come once she was back home actually doing what she had promised.

* * *

Burke stood back, unnoticed as Jenny led her father toward Ebony's pen. He'd tried to get near the critter. He'd seen the men at various times venture close. But only Jenny had been able to gentle the gelding.

Lucky sidled up to him. "If she can tame Ebony, is there any doubt she could tame the land or at least become a part of it?"

"Sing with it, you mean?"

"Something like that."

"I don't know. And it doesn't matter. Her pa has plans for her."

"The man seems reasonable enough. Might be willing to change those plans if he saw something better for her." Lucky sauntered away, leaving Burke struggling with his dreams—dreams he'd buried when Flora ended up in the asylum, but dreams that hadn't died. They'd been part of his plans from the beginning—a family to carry on what he carved out of this land, a woman to share the journey.

Would they ever die?

Did they need to?

He turned into the interior of the barn and perched on the edge of the empty manger. Did God care about what he wanted? Did He take any interest in helping a man find his dream? Win the heart of a woman?

He shook his head. Seemed like such a petty thing

to bother God with. After all, He must be busy with more important things like running the universe and helping seriously ill people.

He had no doubt God had a hand in helping him find Paquette. Several times since then he'd made little requests, almost fearfully. God had not sent angels or done anything spectacular, but always Burke had found the answer after he prayed. Was it coincidence? Or the result of asking?

Jenny fully believed God was concerned with the details of a person's life. He half believed it. Wanted to believe it fully.

But if he did, what would stop him from asking God to allow Jenny to decide to stay? His heart tightened as if squeezed by a miserly fist. Mama cat rubbed against him and he stroked her mindlessly.

He couldn't ask because he feared the answer. Acknowledging love carried an inherent risk. Always there was a danger of losing the loved one. Not necessarily the same way Flora had been lost. But he'd lost his parents. He'd lost Lena. Life carried a risk.

Yes, life carried a risk. And he didn't intend to avoid life because of that. In fact, he welcomed the challenges and risks. It made life worth living.

Why should love be any different? Certainly it was worth whatever risks it came with.

He loved Jenny. With a love as high as the Dakota sky, as wide as the Dakota horizon and as deep as the soil beneath his feet. He had never loved anyone more. Certainly the emotion he felt for Flora was more convenience than this passion wrapping about his heart and binding it with bands of steel.

But what was he to do about it?

Lucky said he thought Mr. Archibald seemed a reasonable man. But would he consider a request from Burke for Jenny's hand a reasonable thing?

His heart overflowing with hope and love, he bowed his head. "Lord God, You are so big, so powerful that it boggles my mind that You would bother with my little problems."

Mama cat meowed and pushed against him, perhaps thinking Burke talked to her. He gently nudged her aside.

"But it seems You're big enough, powerful enough to have time for each of us. So I come to You with one request. Help me find favor with Jenny's pa. Help him see that she belongs out here with me."

That evening after everyone had gone to bed, Jenny pulled out her Bible and looked up the verse Pa had quoted. She read the Psalm. The last two verses seemed to grab her by the chin and pull her attention to them.

"Search me, O God; and know my heart: try me, and know my thoughts: And see if there be any wicked way in me, and lead me in the way everlasting."

The words went round and round in her head until they settled down solidly, forcing her to acknowledge them.

Her love of the prairie did not come from wickedness in her heart. Nor did her love for Burke. Perhaps, if God had made no mistakes in creating her with a heart that sought adventure and new things, He had done so for the express purpose of preparing her to share in such a life as this.

But would Burke withdraw the interest he could not hide if he knew the whole truth about her?

She must find out. She would tell Burke everything, then if he didn't turn away in disgust, she would tell Pa she couldn't honestly marry Ted with her heart yearning after Burke.

She prayed a long time before she fell asleep, asking for guidance and direction in her plan.

Chapter Thirteen

Jenny's heart beat erratically throughout breakfast the next morning as she considered her plan. She'd never confessed the results of her foolhardiness to anyone. Ma and Pa knew, of course. But not even her sisters knew the events of that dreadful day.

She silently prayed throughout the meal and afterwards as she helped clean the kitchen. *Lord, give me strength to be honest.*

Pa returned to fixing things around the house. Miss Morgan sat at the table playing with Meggie. Paquette disappeared to her room. Jenny had no excuse for delay. Didn't want one. She wanted to get it over with and live with the consequences. If Burke turned away in disgust…

During the long night of soul searching she had come to several conclusions. Although certain of her decisions, she did not anticipate her parents' reactions and she grabbed at her stomach as if she could stop the feeling that her entire insides dropped out the bottom. If Burke rejected her after her story, she would have no choice but to return with Pa. Though she would not marry Ted. She would tell Pa she'd sooner be a spinster than marry out of duty. Surely Pa would understand.

Her hope was a fervent plea. Pa would expect her to obey. But she could not. Her heart would never belong to Ted.

"I'm stepping out for a few minutes," she informed Miss Morgan.

"Me come." Meggie started to scramble from the bench.

Miss Morgan caught her but before she could say anything, Jenny bent over and touched Meggie's chin. "Not this time, sweetie. You stay here and play." This was not a time for little girls to be present.

Gathering together her courage, her faith and determination, she stepped outdoors and glanced around wondering where she could find Burke. She'd kept close watch to see if he rode out of the yard and had not seen him but perhaps he'd escaped her notice. She chuckled. He'd have to be invisible for her to miss him. She hadn't taken her gaze from the window for more than a fleeting second or two since he walked out the door after breakfast.

Burke had gone into the barn, left again with

Mama cat meowing at his heels. She'd smiled as he bent and petted the cat. She saw his mouth moving and knew he talked to the animal. Burke was a man strong enough, determined and tough enough to challenge this new land—a land he confessed was unfriendly to most, yet gentle enough to pay an old cat attention and to hold a sad little girl close.

And perhaps to forgive a young woman for her sinfulness.

She bound that hope about her heart and stood listening for anything to indicate his presence. A sound drew her attention and she smiled. Burke whistling as he worked. She headed toward the sound and found him leaning against the handle of a pitchfork, staring into the distance like a man studying his world, planning how to conquer it.

He turned at her approach and smiled, a tentativeness about his eyes. "Hi." Perhaps he expected her to announce she and Pa were leaving to return to their plans…plans that included Ted.

She faltered. What would his response be when she informed him Ted was no longer a part of her plans? Her heart headed for the bottom again at the thought of what else she must tell him.

"Did you need something?"

"Can we talk?"

He hesitated. Caution filled his eyes and then he masked all expression. "Certainly. Want to sit?" He waved toward the wall of the barn and waited for her to arrange herself on the grassy area, her back pressed to the rough boards, then he sat next to her, his legs stretched out before him. He took off his hat, laid it in his lap and tipped his head against the barn.

For a moment neither of them spoke.

She closed her eyes and let the sun warm her. Prayed for guidance and strength.

"What can I do for you?" he prodded.

She sucked in the warm air, filling her lungs endlessly. Still she felt breathless. "You've accused me of letting my father plan my life."

"It's none of my business."

She hoped he'd change his mind about that. "You were right. I—" She'd rehearsed this speech but now couldn't think how to start it. "I thought I had to. Not only because I thought I should obey my parents but because going my own way led me into a pack of trouble."

He shifted slightly, turning so he could watch her as she spoke. Unable to face him, she ducked her head.

"I can see you getting yourself into predicaments." The amusement in his voice caused her to jerk her gaze to his face. She clung to the way his eyes softened as he smiled. "Seems to me you've been heedless of the dangers a few times in our short acquaintance."

"I have not."

"Ebony?"

"I didn't know that was a danger."

"Never crossed your mind. That's what I mean. You don't even acknowledge risks." He said it like it was something she should be proud of.

"That's why I try to always think what Ma or Pa would advise before I act. You see…" She tightened her fists and forced herself to go on. "I learned a very difficult lesson about the folly of not listening."

He nodded, his gaze intent, demanding, waiting.

She ducked her head again and tried to remember how she planned to tell this sordid tale. "I was fifteen when I learned the hard way why I should heed my parents in all things." Almost four years ago and still she fought to make the lesson stick. "I want to tell you about it." To see if he could stand to look at her after her story. "The circus had come to town. Ma and Pa promised to take us the next day but I wanted to see the animals unloaded, the tents put up. I wanted to experience the excitement." Her voice fell to a whisper and for the life of her, she couldn't make it any stronger. "Pa warned me to stay away. Said it was a rough place." She cleared her throat and forced herself to go on. "I disobeyed him and went with some of my classmates."

It had seemed so exciting. They'd laughed as they met away from their homes. The boys pushed each other and roughhoused. She and the other girl giggled and raced after them.

"At first it was fun. To see the tents staked into place and then lifted. They used an elephant to help raise the big top." She'd stared open-mouthed at the lumbering grace of the huge animal and the way it responded to the handler. "We toured the place. Saw the caged lions. Listened to the funny way the people spoke to each other. They seemed to have a language all their own. We watched the booths being set up. It was so exciting." She shuddered.

He touched her hands. She didn't realize how she twisted them until he claimed them and stilled them. "But it didn't end up exciting? Is that what you're telling me?"

"I'm trying to, yes. You see I was so fascinated with the elephant. I said I wanted to see it again. I marched back thinking everyone followed me. The animal was standing with a chain around one leg and munching on hay. Did you know they pick up their food with their trunk and then tuck it into their mouths?"

He squeezed her hands. "Never thought much about it."

"I couldn't tear myself away. I wanted so bad to touch the animal but I didn't dare." She tried to swallow but her throat wouldn't work. She opened her mouth and sucked hard at the still, waiting air. "The handler noticed my interest. 'Want to touch me beastie?' He was a big man with a red beard, and eyes that seemed to see right through me. I knew I should say no but I could not. My foolish desire to experience everything, you know. I giggled and said I would. 'Give me your hand and stay close to me.' I only hesitated a moment. Then I let him pull me forward. 'Sheba, meet a new friend,' he crooned and the elephant lifted its trunk and reached for me. It was like touching a snake. Only warm." She gasped for air and forced herself to calm down.

"I looked back to tell my friends and that's when I realized I was alone. They hadn't followed. And that's when the man jerked me around and—" She tried to keep her voice steady. "He pulled me against him and touched me—" Her cheeks felt about to melt off her face at her revulsion at the way he had touched forbidden places. "He said he could show me things a lot more exciting than an old elephant. I tried to pull away but he laughed—an awful sound."

She clamped her hands over her ears as if she could somehow block the memory from her mind.

"He forced me into a little tent. I tried to get away." The words came out in hot gasps. "He only laughed again. Wouldn't stop laughing. He—" She clutched at the material of her dress at her neck and twisted. "He grabbed my dress and tore it."

She wrapped her arms across her chest. "He touched me."

Her skin felt cold and clammy. He'd pushed her backward. "He had a cot in the corner." The cold metal of the frame had pressed into her calves. Hard, unforgiving, icy like winter iron. Press your tongue to it and stick. She couldn't get away. His huge body blocked her escape. His hands were everywhere. She couldn't get warm and vibrated with the chill that burrowed into the marrow of her bones and encased her heart. Her lungs cried for air but there was none. Only a contrast of hot and cold, fear and coarse laughter. She tried to squirm away. Fought like a cornered animal. Scratched. He caught her hands and laughed.

Trapped her.

Her teeth rattled as fear and loathing and remembrance sucked at her until she felt nothing else.

"Jenny?" He touched her shoulder. Gentle.

She shrank back.

"Jenny. I won't hurt you. Ever."

Not the growling sneer of the man. Burke. His voice soft, kind.

"Jenny. It's okay. Whatever happened, it's okay." He edged closer and took her hand.

Her fingers remained stiff and unyielding in his

grasp. She couldn't respond to his touch. But she couldn't pull away either. God help her but she needed to feel a connection with him. For years she had shut her heart to feeling anything but determination to obey.

"I haven't finished my story." Her words shook as badly as she did.

"You don't need to."

"I do." He must hear it all and then decide for himself who she was.

"He had to release me to reach for his trousers. It was all I needed. I escaped and raced for the flap and right into Pa's arms. He had come looking for me. He took off his jacket and wrapped it around me and made me wait outside. I don't know what he said. All I know is the sheriff arrested the man and he was sent to jail."

"And you ended up afraid of doing anything risky. Afraid to make a decision apart from your parents."

She nodded. It was true. She feared her own thoughts and actions.

He slipped his arm across her shoulders and pressed her close. She didn't realize how badly she shook until he held her against him, catching the vibrations of her body in his grasp and calming them.

Burke fought an urge to stand up and bellow an angry protest. He hoped the man suffered his just

deserts in some rotten jail cell. Only her quick thinking had prevented her from being violated in the worst
possible way. The disgusting actions of the man had
nevertheless violated her in other ways. Filled her
with shame. Quenched her bold spirit. Made her see
it as a bad thing.

He held her close, careful not to do anything that
would make her feel threatened, absorbing her shud-
ders into his own body.

"So you see why I have felt I should let Pa decide
my future."

Actually, he didn't but how was he to explain that
to her? Her trauma was real, as were her fears about
making another mistake. "You were a foolish child.
You are now a responsible, wiser adult. Even so, foolish child or not, you were not responsible for how that
man acted. Don't you think it's time to stop blaming
yourself?"

She grew still as if considering his words.

This was one time he needed God's help. And
felt sure he could ask for and receive it. *Lord God,
you see her injured spirit. Heal it. And if I can say
anything to help, please give me the words.*

"What I see is a child of fifteen, excited, natu-
rally enough, about a circus, and an evil man who
did wrong. And now I see a young woman who is
adventuresome and eager, trying to deny those God-
given attributes."

"God-given? Do you really think so?"

He chuckled. "Are you not the one who taught me God is interested in the details of our lives? That He not only sees the big things but the little? Now I'm not saying you're unimportant, but if small details and big events are equal in His scheme of things, would you not then accept that He who made the world and everything in it and declared it good, does not think the same about you? Does He not declare His work good?"

She shifted so she could look into his face without leaving his embrace. "Burke, you really believe that?"

He smiled down at her, loving her like he never thought possible. "Don't you?" *Thank you God for giving me words that help.*

"For everyone else. Not for me. Though I am getting closer. Yesterday I finally acknowledged that perhaps God made no mistake in how He made me."

She met his eyes openly as if inviting him to see her wholly, completely, with no secrets between them. He searched past the places he'd been before, wondering what this meant.

She pushed away, slipped from under his arm and shifted around to face him squarely.

He ached a protest, feeling more than her physical withdrawal.

"What do you think of Miss Morgan as a nanny?"

Her question caught him by surprise. When had anything about their discussion been about a nanny? "She'll do. Why? Do you have some concerns?"

"No. She seems adequate."

"But?"

She pulled in air hard enough to flutter his hair. "It's just…" She ducked her head and didn't finish.

He caught her chin and lifted her head. For a moment she kept her eyelids lowered, then realizing his patient waiting, slowly opened her eyes and met his gaze. His heart leapt for his throat at the hungry longing he saw. "It's just what?"

"Well—" She lowered her gaze then jerked it up and watched him with a demanding expression. "I wondered if I might reconsider and ask for the position of nanny." Her words came out in a rush and she stared, eager and excited as she waited for his response.

He dropped his finger, sat back against the barn wall.

She looked disappointed. "Of course, if that doesn't suit you…."

It didn't suit. He didn't want her as a nanny. He wanted more. So much more. But first he must talk to her father. "Have you mentioned this to your pa?"

"Not yet. I thought I'd see what you thought first."

"Seems he's rather set on you returning with him."

"I know." She sounded so disheartened. "I guess you can understand his concern."

His insides rebelled at the defeat in his voice. "No, I'm afraid I don't. What does he have to be concerned about?" He leaned close, wanting to make this very clear. "Jenny, you are a strong young woman. One of the few I feel with certainty who could face this rough land and survive." She soaked up his words, drank of the assurance he offered. He leaned closer and gently kissed her. Rejoiced when she didn't jerk away in fright. He lingered only a second, despite the demands of his heart. "I'll speak to your pa."

"I'll speak to him, too."

He wanted to linger, enjoy this quiet connection they had so recently reached, but someone called from the barn and her pa answered. It was time to get on with the pressing issues of life.

Jenny crossed the yard. Her heart felt scrubbed inside and out. Burke hadn't shrunk away from her. He'd pulled her close and held her. Always she had felt a little dirty, soiled by what happened. Her parents had forbidden it to be mentioned. Not that she ever wanted to talk about it. But telling Burke had left her feeling cleansed and whole. *Thank you, God.*

Pa sat on the veranda watching her approach.

Her steps slowed at the way he looked. Had she done something wrong? Besides disobey his instruction not to speak of the incident.

"You have that look in your eyes," he said.

She faltered as if she'd been caught doing something inappropriate. She realized she always felt like she was being accused—not Pa's fault but by her guilty reaction.

She plunked down beside him. "I told Burke about going to the circus."

"Why would you do that?" His words were soft but faintly accusing.

She couldn't say the real reason—that she hoped he would say it made no difference. That he found her acceptable as a nanny. Perhaps more. Oh, how she longed for more. "He was always mocking me for letting you choose my future husband. I wanted him to understand why I did."

"I see. And what was his response?"

"He didn't call me a fallen woman or anything."

"Has anyone else?" A faint hurt tone came to his voice.

"Pa, I've always felt dirty. Defiled."

"I hope you don't think that's how your ma and I felt. We blamed ourselves for not warning you about such men. We only wanted to shelter you."

She understood that. "It was my own fault for letting my curiosity and wildness control my actions."

She sucked in air, wanting to explain more. "I've always felt anything that excited me or filled me with joy was wrong and would lead to something bad."

Pa hung his head. "I never meant to make you afraid. And certainly never wanted to quench your spirit. Only guide it into a safe channel."

"I know, Pa. But there is something you must understand. Something I've learned about myself out here. You assured me God doesn't make mistakes when He creates us. 'We are fearfully and wonderfully made.' For a long time I've wondered if I was the exception."

"No, daughter—"

"Let me finish. Last night I took a good hard look at what I was becoming. And I didn't think it was what God meant me to be. Burke says it takes a special kind of person to be a pioneer. Women, especially, find it hard because they miss the comforts of home and find the prairie lonely and empty. I don't. I love the challenge." She faced her father squarely. "Pa, I believe God has uniquely equipped me to be one of those who conquers this land." She grabbed his wrists as if she could communicate her urgency through her touch. "I don't want to go back with you. I can't marry Ted."

He looked as if she'd stabbed him.

"Pa, it isn't anything to do with you and Ma. I feel whole here. I am excited about the challenges this land presents. I love the wind and the wide-open spaces. Pa…." Her voice fell to an agonized whisper. "I want you to release me from my promise to marry Ted. I want your blessing to stay here."

"But you agreed." Pa paused as if considering his words. "I fear you are letting your heart rule your head."

"Not rule it, Pa. I've finally learned to be happy with who I am. Can't you see that and allow it?" she spoke gently, not wanting to disappoint her father but knowing she much be all she was created to be.

Pa sighed heavily and pushed to his feet. "I need to consider your request. I think I'll take a little walk and seek God's guidance."

She watched him go. It hurt to disappoint him but she could no longer be content to be a meek shadow of herself, hiding behind her father's wishes. She prayed God would intervene. That she could begin to rejoice in the woman she was created to be.

Her heart cracked open and bled a bit. She would stay as a nanny but she wanted so much more. She wanted to share every aspect of Burke's life as his wife and helpmate.

Chapter Fourteen

As Jenny crossed the yard to speak to her father, Burke prayed the man would set her free to be all she was meant to be. From the corner of the barn he watched them talking.

When the man walked away on his own, he prayed some more and waited. He tried to busy himself so Lucky wouldn't offer any comments, but there was little he could do without fear of missing Mr. Archibald's return to the yard.

"Little lady got your ropes in a knot?" Lucky said.

"Nope." He rearranged the reins and harnesses hanging near the door and kept his head down while glancing in the direction Jenny's pa had gone.

"Won't be getting unknotted until you admit what's right in front of your nose."

"Maybe I already have."

"Huh. How's that?" The man abandoned all pretense of work and came to hover at Burke's side.

"I'm waiting for her pa to come back so I can talk to him."

Lucky grabbed his hat and slapped it against his thigh. "Yahoo!" His yell sent the pigeons in the loft into a flurry. "Boss, the boys and I figured you were going to let a good thing go just because of what happened to Flora." He clapped Burke on the back. "Nice to see you come to your senses."

Burke rolled his eyes. "Nice of you and the boys to be so concerned about my affairs."

Lucky chortled. "We prefer to work for a happy man." And still chortling, he sauntered away.

"There's been nothing decided yet. I have to talk to her pa."

Lucky turned to face him. "The man looks to be reasonable. And what's more, he cares about his daughter's happiness." He waved and headed for the bunkhouse.

Nice to realize he had the support of the men.

Mr. Archibald appeared on the trail. Now to face the man who had a say in Jenny's future. *Lord God, help me find the right words.*

He waited a few more minutes then strode out to meet Jenny's father. "Sir, I would like to talk to you."

"Go ahead."

"I know you have plans for your daughter."

"I only want her to be happy."

Exactly the opening he needed. "Will she be, back East? Her heart seeks adventure."

Mr. Archibald stopped and faced him squarely, his eyes boring into Burke, demanding nothing but honesty. "Will she be happy here?"

Burke faltered, remembering Flora. He swallowed hard. "I would do my best to make her so, but I have to be honest and tell you I failed in the past."

Mr. Archibald's eyes narrowed. "Perhaps you should tell me about it before I render a decision."

"I'm sure Jenny has told you I sent for Flora Larson intending to marry her. I knew her before I came west and we corresponded for several years. However—" He went on to confess he'd expected too much of her. "I blame myself for her current condition." His voice revealed the degree of his pain. "As do her parents."

Jenny's pa squeezed Burke's shoulder. "Son, I expect your guilt is misplaced. From what I've heard at the store, I understand that even before Flora came out here she had spent some time convalescing."

Burke knew he meant because of her mental condition.

Mr. Archibald seemed to consider his next words. "I don't normally like to repeat things I overhear, but in this case I think I should. I believe her parents hoped the change of scenery would help her. Unfortunately, it didn't. But they have no right to blame you. Her aunt and grandmother are in asylums as well."

It wasn't his fault. Flora had been weak in her mind before she came west. Seems there was a weakness in the family. A great burden of guilt slipped from his shoulders. "Thank you for telling me. I've blamed myself, wondered if any woman could live this life."

Jenny's pa laughed. "I expect you've had cause to change your mind on that score."

Burke grinned widely, his insides bubbling with pleasure at the memories crowding his mind. "Jenny has challenged my opinion more than once."

The man studied him long and hard. "Are you asking for her hand in marriage?"

"With your permission, sir. I understand I don't live up to your expectations of what you want for Jenny's future, but I love her and we seem…" He struggled to explain how he felt as if she pulled up beside him and cheered him on the way, bent her shoulder to the challenges. "She would be a great encouragement to me. And I would do my best to see her life is full of joy." He glanced past the man to the rolling grassland. "I haven't mentioned this to her yet. I wanted your permission first."

"Son, you have my permission and blessing." Mr. Archibald held out his hand and Burke shook it firmly.

Jenny watched the men talking, saw them shake hands. "Oh Lord, let Pa agree to let me stay." She waited for Pa to return to the house.

"Jenny, my dear, I wanted only to protect you, assure your happiness but I see you are ready to determine what that requires on your own."

She realized she'd forgotten to breathe and sucked in air. "You aren't holding me to my promise to return home and marry Ted?"

"Doesn't seem to me it would be quite fair to Ted." He chuckled. "Now go see your young man and talk to him."

She stretched up and kissed Pa on the cheek. "Thank you, Pa. I love you."

Pa hugged her quickly. "I love you, too, Pepper." He released her.

She spun from his arms and rushed toward Burke, who waited on the path. It took all her rigid self-control not to fling herself into his arms. Was he going to ask her to stay as a nanny or—she faltered a step—share his life completely and wholly?

His eyes invited her. Suddenly she felt wooden. Her steps slowed as he took off his hat and pushed a hand through his hair.

His lovely shiny black hair. She'd admired it from

the beginning. It had grown some since then, which only made him more handsome. She drank in every detail. His lean strength, the way he stood as if he owned the land and dared anyone to challenge him about it. The way his muscles strained at his shirt-sleeves as he crossed his arms. She would never get tired of looking at him. She scrubbed her lips together, surprised at how numb they were. Without words she prayed for God's blessing on her love for Burke.

Of their own accord her feet moved forward until she had only to lift her hand to touch him.

Love made her ache to do so.

Uncertainty stifled her reaction. She didn't know what his plans were.

He took her hand and pulled it through his arm, patting her fingers to the warm strength of his fore-arm and keeping his palm on top of her hand. "Shall we walk?"

She nodded, unable to speak past the expectant lump in her throat.

He turned them toward the corrals. They passed Ebony's pen. He whinnied at Jenny then snorted and reared at her escort.

She chuckled. "It's only pretend."

"He figures he belongs to you and he's not willing to share."

The regretful note in his voice sent her nerves into eager anticipation.

They skirted the barn and returned to the spot they had shared a few hours earlier. Once they were out of sight of the house and bunkhouse, he stopped and turned toward her, his hands gentle on her upper arms.

Slowly, her heart crowding her ribs so she had trouble breathing, she lifted her face to him.

A smile lifted his mouth and creased his eyes. He studied her slowly as if memorizing every detail of her features.

Her skin warmed as his gaze checked her eyebrows, admired her cheeks, lingered on her lips until she ached for him to end this misery of waiting, and kiss her.

Then slowly, almost reluctantly, he brought his gaze to her eyes. She floated in his look.

"Your Pa has given me his blessing to ask you to stay."

Stay? That's all. "As a nanny?"

He blinked, surprised, then chuckled softly, a sound that played harp strings along her nerves. "I hope much more than that. Jenny—" He caught her chin in his fingers, his touch making music in every corner of her heart. "I knew you were different the first time I laid eyes on you."

Remembering his dire warning that day and his

insistence for days after her arrival that she didn't belong here, she found the ability to quirk her brows. "Sure could have fooled me."

He lifted one shoulder and looked sheepish, making her want to stroke his cheek and assure him she understood.

"I tried to convince us both, but I'm so grateful you didn't pay me any heed because I can't imagine life without you." He swallowed hard and she perceived his nervousness, his uncertainty.

She touched his shoulder. The twitch of his muscles as he reacted to her touch thrilled her. He was a man who would stand strong through the fiercest storm. Her touch seemed to drive away his hesitation.

"Jenny, I love you. I want to marry you and spend the rest of my life with you."

Her heart exploded inside her chest with such force she couldn't speak, couldn't breathe, couldn't move.

"Jenny, will you marry me?"

Blood flowed again, warm and vibrant, just as her life would be. "Burke Edwards, I love you heart and soul and mind. Of course I will marry you."

His face filled with such joy she almost couldn't look at him. To know and share such love the rest of her life…. It was more than she could believe possible.

"Jenny," he whispered, his words round with awe. "I am the happiest man alive."

And then he finally kissed her, his lips warm and promising. She wrapped her arms about him and gave herself freely to the kiss, silently vowing to honor and cherish him the rest of her life.

Finally, he pulled back. "I love you so much."

She stroked his cheek then.

He turned his face and pressed his lips to her palm.

"I have loved you since I saw you on the train, even though I feared it was wrong." Her words sang from her lips.

"Nothing about our love has ever been wrong or ever will be. Not with God as our partner."

He drew her to the spot where they'd sat before, and they sat side by side. He draped his arm over her shoulder and pulled her close. She snuggled against his chest, feeling the rise and fall of each breath and hearing the beat of his heart beneath her ear.

She had found a safe place.

They talked of their hopes and plans and dreams. She loved him before, but as they opened their hearts to one another something eternal and precious grew between them, making them one in spirit.

They talked until the sun came round and blasted them in the face.

"Can you believe we've been here all afternoon?" Burke said.

"We'll enjoy many more times like this, sharing our joys…and no doubt some sorrows." Her heart rejoiced to know that whatever came, they would find strength through being together.

He kissed her nose and cheeks then claimed her mouth for several seconds before he pulled her to her feet. Hand in hand they wandered back to the house.

Ebony repeated his performance of acting spooky. He stopped as soon as they passed and hurried to the fence, whinnying for Jenny to stop and pet him. She laughed. "He's determined to be friends with no one but me."

"He's yours."

She drew to a halt. "You're giving him to me?"

"Might as well." He tweaked her chin. "He thinks he belongs to you already."

"Can I ride him?"

Burke grinned. "Do you know how to ride?"

"No, but I can learn."

His eyes flashed with amusement. "Maybe you could start on something more gentle and if you prove yourself a capable horsewoman—"

She didn't let him finish. "Not if—when—I prove my ability."

"You will always face a challenge with the idea of

conquering whatever obstacle lies in your way, won't you?" He pulled her to his side as they resumed their journey to the house.

She didn't respond right away as she sorted her thoughts. "God made me this way and I am learning to be grateful for the strengths He gave me."

He hugged her and paused to kiss her upturned mouth. "I will spend the rest of my life being grateful."

Epilogue

Pa's one stipulation had been they go back to Center City to marry, allowing Ma to meet Jenny's future husband, so they boarded the train heading east, Miss Morgan accompanying them as she also returned home.

Paquette had miraculously recovered all her faculties and would cook for the men while Burke and Jenny were away. Paquette had shuffled up to Jenny one evening before their departure. "I leave after you back, me?"

Jenny heard the doubt and fear in the older woman's voice. She hugged the tiny woman. "I hope you won't. I want you to stay. I need you to teach me everything I need to know about living on the prairie. Besides, don't you think we work well as a team?"

Paquette beamed with joy. "We good, us. I stay."

Pa had wired Ma warning her of their arrival,

suggesting she prepare for a wedding as quickly as possible.

Ma met them at the station. Jenny flew into her arms. "Ma, it's good to see you."

Ma hugged her hard. "Am I to lose you to a wild man from the west?"

"'Fraid so, Ma. But I think you'll like him." She signaled Burke forward. "Ma, here he is. The man from the west."

Burke took Ma's hand in both his. "Mrs. Archibald, I want to thank you for raising such a beautiful, sweet woman."

Ma beamed and darted a look at Jenny that said she approved.

A week later she stood at Burke's side in the manse and faced the preacher. Her sister, Mary, and her husband stood up with them. The week had been packed with visiting family and showing Burke the store. Jenny smiled as she recalled their first visit. Ted stood behind the counter, his head high, his nose tilted slightly upward. Jenny hated to face him. She'd never spoken a word of promise to him, but she knew Pa had discussed the future and Ted had reason to think she might be at his side.

Burke, sensing her hesitation, strode forward. "You're the efficient young man I've heard so much about."

Ted's nose lowered and he smiled. He liked to be recognized as efficient and forward thinking. After that, the meeting went easily and Ted hid any disappointment at her upcoming marriage. Jenny hoped he'd find someone who touched his heart as much as Burke did hers.

She smiled up at Burke, knowing her heart filled her eyes and revealed the depths of her love. She still found it difficult to contain. She could hardly wait to get back to the ranch where she could run into the prairie and shout her joy without causing people to turn and stare.

Burke met her smile with dark, calm steadiness. Her eyes watered at the look he gave her, full of promise and tenderness.

Then the preacher spoke words that bound them together until death. "I now pronounce you man and wife. You may kiss your bride."

Burke did so, his hunger and love matched by her own.

"From this day forth," he murmured against her ear as they ended the kiss, aware of their audience.

Her eyes overflowed with joy. "Our great adventure is about to begin."

He laughed. "I thought it already had. You've led me on a merry chase already."

"No more than you've led me." She hugged his arm and pressed close to him. She would never stop being grateful for his quiet acceptance of what she'd always thought was the worst moment of her life. It no longer controlled her thoughts and actions. She felt free and fulfilled. A feeling that would no doubt multiply over and over as she shared her life with Burke.

Ma had insisted on preparing tea for them. Only family and a few friends attended as Burke was insistent they leave on the next train.

Sadness mingled with her joy as she kissed her family good-bye. Burke held Meggie in his arms and waited, patient and understanding of her tears.

Pa took them to the station. Here was her last and hardest good-bye. He held her tight. "Be happy, Pepper."

He shook Burke's hand. "I expect she'll make your life interesting."

Burke chuckled. "I'm counting on it."

Pa reached under the seat, pulled out a long package and handed it to Jenny. "A good-bye gift. Open it on the train."

Jenny's throat grew so tight she could hardly speak. "Thank you for everything, Pa."

"All aboard!"

They hurried into the car and found seats where they could see Pa and wave to him until he was out of sight.

Burke caught her hand.

"You'll be back often for visits. I promise."

She faced her husband. "Thank you, but I expect I'll hate to be away from the ranch very much. I might miss out on something." Meggie, exhausted, fell asleep in Burke's arms.

"Aren't you going to open the parcel?" Burke nodded toward the package Pa had given her.

She undid the string and folded back the paper. At first she didn't know what it was—red silk and sticks. Then she laughed. "It's a kite." A note lay on top and she opened it. "Go and fly like you were meant to."

"I once told Pa the prairie wind made me want to be a kite and fly free." Her voice thickened with emotion.

His eyes grew troubled. "I hope you won't find marriage clips your wings."

She laughed. "Sharing my life with you will be the biggest adventure ever. I feel like I am flying every time you kiss me."

"Me, too. And it's a wonderful sensation." He pulled her close and kissed her briefly. "I'll do it well and thoroughly when we get home."

Home. The nicest word in the world, Jenny decided.

Burke tucked her head against his shoulder. "Did I tell you how I thank God every day for bringing you to me? You taught me He cares about every detail of my life."

He had told her but she would never get tired of hearing it. "You have given me so much. Besides your love, the greatest gift you've given me is the assurance that I can be who I am without fear of criticism."

He kissed her again, briefly, gently. "I wouldn't want you to be anything else."

* * * * *

Dear Reader,

For years I have been fascinated with the way events from our past have such an influence on our lives. Some events are real and horrible, some are subtle (like an insult that made a negative impact) and some are even imagined, based on wrong interpretations and faulty information. In this story, Jenny's past contains an event that has shaped her life. It has colored the way she thinks, how she perceives comments—even who she plans to marry.

I think all of us have past issues that need to be addressed. Perhaps in reading Jenny and Burke's story, you, my dear reader, will find encouragement to confront something in your past and allow God to heal it.

That is my prayer for you.

I love to hear from my readers. You can contact me and check out my other books at www.lindaford.org.

Blessings,

Linda Ford

QUESTIONS FOR DISCUSSION

1. Burke is sure the prairies will drive Jenny home. What was there about the prairies that could frighten a person?

2. What did Jenny find about the prairies that charmed her?

3. Are there times when you can't understand how someone could have such an opposing view from yours on some topic? Is it possible you can both be right?

4. Do you think Jenny's determination to obey her parents was right or wrong? Why?

5. What roles did Paquette and the ranch hands play in helping Jenny and Burke to find love?

6. Jenny suffered a frightening event in her past. How did it shape the way she viewed herself and how she made decisions?

7. Have you suffered events that affect you today? Have you found someone you can share these with?

8. There are several things that enabled Jenny to confront her past and find healing. What were they?

9. Can you think of other things that might have helped?

10. Is there a particular verse in this story that brought you comfort? Are there other verses you would have applied in this situation?

11. Burke, too, had experiences that shaped him. Which one do you think was the most influential?

12. How would you have handled his situation if it were you?

13. What conclusion did Burke reach about God because of his experiences?

14. Would you have felt the same way? Why or why not?

15. How did Burke learn to trust God in the events of his life?

16. How do you foresee the future for Burke and Jenny? Will it be happy?

HISTORICAL

TITLES AVAILABLE NEXT MONTH

Available February 8, 2011

REQUEST YOUR FREE BOOKS!

2 FREE INSPIRATIONAL NOVELS
PLUS 2
FREE
MYSTERY GIFTS

Love Inspired
HISTORICAL
INSPIRATIONAL HISTORICAL ROMANCE

YES! Please send me 2 FREE Love Inspired® Historical novels and my 2 FREE mystery gifts (gifts are worth about $10). After receiving them, if I don't wish to receive any more books, I can return the shipping statement marked "cancel". If I don't cancel, I will receive 4 brand-new novels every other month and be billed just $4.24 per book in the U.S. or $4.74 per book in Canada. That's a saving of over 20% off the cover price. It's quite a bargain! Shipping and handling is just 50¢ per book.* I understand that accepting the 2 free books and gifts places me under no obligation to buy anything. I can always return a shipment and cancel at any time. Even if I never buy another book, the two free books and gifts are mine to keep forever.

102/302 IDN E7QD

Name	(PLEASE PRINT)
Address	Apt. #
City	State/Prov.	Zip/Postal Code

Signature (if under 18, a parent or guardian must sign)

Mail to **Steeple Hill Reader Service:**
IN U.S.A.: P.O. Box 1867, Buffalo, NY 14240-1867
IN CANADA: P.O. Box 609, Fort Erie, Ontario L2A 5X3

Not valid for current subscribers to Love Inspired Historical books.

Want to try two free books from another series?
Call 1-800-873-8635 or visit www.morefreebooks.com.

* Terms and prices subject to change without notice. Prices do not include applicable taxes. Sales tax applicable in N.Y. Canadian residents will be charged applicable provincial taxes and GST. Offer not valid in Quebec. This offer is limited to one order per household. All orders subject to approval. Credit or debit balances in a customer's account(s) may be offset by any other outstanding balance owed by or to the customer. Please allow 4 to 6 weeks for delivery. Offer available while quantities last.

Your Privacy: Steeple Hill Books is committed to protecting your privacy. Our Privacy Policy is available online at www.SteepleHill.com or upon request from the Reader Service. From time to time we make our lists of customers available to reputable third parties who may have a product or service of interest to you. If you would prefer we not share your name and address, please check here. ☐

Help us get it right—We strive for accurate, respectful and relevant communications. To clarify or modify your communication preferences, visit us at www.ReaderService.com/consumerchoice.

LIH10R

Love Inspired
HISTORICAL

INSPIRATIONAL HISTORICAL ROMANCE

Dr. Ben Drake has always held a special place in his heart for strays. The ultimate test of his compassion comes when the fragile beauty at his door is revealed to be his brother's widow. Callie could expose the Drakes' darkest family secrets but just one look at her and Ben knows he can't turn her away—not when he can lead her to true love and God's forgiving grace.

Rocky Mountain Redemption

by
PAMELA NISSEN

*Available February
wherever books are sold.*

www.SteepleHill.com

Steeple
Hill®

Love Inspired
SUSPENSE
RIVETING INSPIRATIONAL ROMANCE

TEXAS RANGER JUSTICE
★ ★ ★ ★ ★ ★ ★ ★ ★ ★ ★ ★ ★ ★ ★ ★ ★ ★ ★ ★

Keeping the Lone Star State safe

Follow the men and women of the Texas Rangers,
as they risk their lives to help save others,
with

DAUGHTER OF TEXAS by **Terri Reed**
January 2011

BODY OF EVIDENCE by **Lenora Worth**
February 2011

FACE OF DANGER by **Valerie Hansen**
March 2011

TRAIL OF LIES by **Margaret Daley**
April 2011

THREAT OF EXPOSURE by **Lynette Eason**
May 2011

OUT OF TIME by **Shirlee McCoy**
June 2011

Available wherever books are sold.

www.SteepleHill.com

Steeple
Hill®